Hannah

CHRIS KENISTON
USA TODAY BESTSELLING AUTHOR

Indie House Publishing

Indie House Publishing

BOOKS BY CHRIS KENISTON

Aloha Series
Aloha Texas
Almost Paradise
Mai Tai Marriage
Dive Into You
Shell Game
Look of Love
Love by Design
Love Walks In
Waikiki Wedding

Surf's Up Flirts
(Aloha Series Companions)
Shall We Dance
Love on Tap
Head Over Heels
Perfect Match
Just One Kiss
It Had to Be You

Honeymoon Series
Honeymoon for One
Honeymoon for Three

Family Secrets Novels
Champagne Sisterhood
The Homecoming
Hope's Corner

Farraday Country

Adam

Brooks

Connor

Declan

Ethan

Finn

Grace

Hannah

Ian

Jamison

ACKNOWLEDGEMENTS

There are days when I know without my friends these books would never get written. Hannah is no exception. My author friends are wonderful in sharing their expertise.

Liz Lipperman once again helped me out with whatever I don't know about blood thinners.

Idea woman extraordinaire, Cindy Dees, thanks for giving me the twist for this book and the next.

If not for Kathy Ivan and the steady use of her home and her brainstorming, this book would still be on my laptop half written.

Once again JM Madden to the rescue on horse stuff I should know by now and don't.

And first time helper author Vanessa Kier who had the good graces to know way more than me about adaptive riding and was willing to share. You are my hero!

Something has to be said to my cheering section, yes my family, but the readers who take the time to send me notes, or post on my pages, or leave reviews telling me how much you love the Farradays. Best motivation ever to think up new and fun stories for you.

Y'all ROCK !

Thank you for reading Hannah!

CHAPTER ONE

"What the hell are you doing up there?"

Not expecting her cousin Connor to be finished with the horses so soon, Hannah Siobhan Farraday almost teetered off the stone pillar at his bark. "Taking in the view." She gripped the post more tightly. "What does it look like I'm doing?"

"Like you're getting ready to dive off my wall and break your neck."

"Says the man who swung from an oil rig for a living."

Connor looked over to the crew chief he'd hired to replace the hundred-year-old gate arch with the new stable name. "Where's the rest of the crew?"

"Running late." The balding middle-aged man with a rounded gut barely glanced at Connor. "This little lady is helping with set up."

Somehow Hannah doubted holding the end of a measuring tape constituted set up, but when the guy was bumbling around waiting for his crew, she figured the least she could do was hop up and help hold the flat end of the tape in place. Heaven knew there was no way this guy would be able to hop up onto anything higher than an ant mound. She tipped her head from her cousin to the back of the large truck. "Have you looked?"

Concern fell from Connor's face as his gaze landed on the massive new arch. A slow, sure grin tipped one side of his mouth skyward and eased across, lifting the other corner up to match. "Sweet."

"Yeah." As excited as she was about the new stables, anyone would think she had a stake in it other than family pride. She couldn't have been more excited about the new stables and the equine program if she'd owned the place. The opportunity to be in on the ground floor and bring change, hope, to people who couldn't normally have access or afford it was worth walking away from all she'd begun to build in Dallas. Though she'd like to think the reputation she'd begun to build for herself would follow her.

Clipboard in hand, the crew chief scribbled something down and then handed Hannah the metallic casing of the measuring tape. "Here, you grab this end and tell me what you read." Taking hold of the edge of the tape, he crossed the expanse of the entryway and balanced on the first rung of the ladder against the stone column and set the tape at the midpoint of the support posts. "Whatcha got?"

"Two hundred and sixty four on the nose."

"Good. Good," the man muttered to no one in particular.

She'd have thought with a project this size they would have measured and cross-measured a few hundred times already, but one more time wasn't going to kill anyone. Rolling in the length of the tape, she nodded at the guy and spun about on the narrow wall.

"Here." Connor moved forward and raised an arm. "Let me help you."

"I got up here without you. I can get down on my own steam too." Shimmying around, she toed a ridge of stone and climbed down the wall as easily as she'd scurried up.

Shaking his head, Connor chuckled, his smile still consuming his face. "Don't know why I bother."

Hannah leaned in and kissed her cousin on the cheek. Even though the West Texas Farradays and the Hill Country Farradays didn't live close at all by normal people's standards, they still spent enough time with each other to consider themselves more like siblings than cousins. "Cause you love me."

Connor laughed outright. "There is that."

Kicking up dust as it turned off the main road, the winch truck with the remaining crew pulled up and parked beside the massive ironwork. The gleam in Connor's eyes had the hairs on Hannah's arm standing on edge. Her cousin had dreamed of this day most of his life and she could hardly stand the anticipation. Yes, building the arenas and corrals and additional stables for the initial equine therapy program had been a satisfying part of seeing the dream come true, but this—the traditional iron banner—this was the icing on the cake.

The process of lifting an ironwork that weighed several hundred pounds was not quick, or even all that complex, yet Hannah and Connor stood rooted in place, riveted by the slow-moving action. Content to see history in the making. Coming from the direction of town, the stable truck with Catherine, Connor's wife, pulled up behind them.

Doors slammed and Catherine hurried up to her husband, easily curling in beside him. "I thought I might miss it."

Connor draped an arm across his wife's shoulder and pulled her in close. It was really sweet the way her cousins gave their all to the women in their lives. For some, like Adam, it had taken longer than the others, but once a Farraday man found his mate, she got 100 percent of what he had to give. The trick in the next decade or so for Hannah would be finding a man of her own who could live up to her cousins.

"And here we go," Catherine whispered.

The large piece of art descended over the entry and with a little shuffling by the men on either side, the ends slipped into place and Hannah's heart leapt as surely as if Capaill Stables was hers.

For a few more minutes the three of them stood just inside the open gates and stared up as the workers completed the task of securing the new name in place.

"Looks pretty good," Catherine whispered.

"Better than good," Hannah added.

"Granddad would be pleased," Catherine said.

Connor dragged his gaze from the old Gaelic name his father had aptly suggested for the ranch, Capaill, and studied his wife's face. "You think so?"

"I really do." Catherine beamed. "He loved this place. Took

pride in its history and I know deep down, if he were here, he'd be thrilled to see the Brennans and Farradays come together on this land."

"And that," Hannah rubbed her hands together, "is my cue to get back to work. I want to take the new Fjord filly for a ride. Seems a bit skittish to me so far. Calls for a nice long visit, just the two of us."

"You don't think she'll be good for therapy?" Catherine asked. The only reason they'd taken on this shorter, stockier breed was for its ability to carry heavier weight and because the height would make it easier for volunteers to lead the horse. The last thing anyone wanted was for the mare to turn out to be a poor fit for the new program.

"We'll see. Could simply need adjusting to the new environment." At least that was the story she was sticking to. Finding a good therapy horse was a bit like finding a good man; they might look pretty handsome at first sight, but once you get to know them, they could easily become more of a problem than a prize.

• • • •

There was something to be said for the comfort of plush leather seats in a superior made luxury car. Too bad Dale Johnson couldn't say the same for the two wheels underneath him. At first, driving out of town, the roar of the engine beneath him and the wind in his face felt fantastic. The sense of freedom had been missing too damn long from his life. The long-forgotten sensations almost made up for the mess he'd gotten himself into. Almost.

Now that he'd been on these never-ending Texas back roads for more hours than he cared to count, he wished he'd bought himself a secondhand car instead of this two-wheeled kickstand that would not require frequent refueling like a car, gas station cameras be damned.

Of course, maybe after a good night's sleep on a real mattress, caution will win out again. Then again, he was going to need a lot more than a single night's sleep to put his life back in order—and his back. According to his calculations and the last road sign he'd seen, he should be arriving in Tuckers Bluff in about another hour or so. What he needed now was to get off this machine for at least a few minutes and walk off the numbness taking over the few body parts that didn't hurt like an SOB. It hadn't taken long after leaving Dallas to realize he would not be getting away with riding for a hours without stopping. At this point, with every added mile, his back strenuously voted for more rest stops. Too bad he couldn't plug the heating pad into the engine. Slowing to the side of the road, he came to a stop and gingerly eased his way off the bike. A whole hell of a lot slower than he would have liked, but at least he was moving. Sure beat the alternative.

A swig of cool water went an even longer way to easing the burn in his throat, if not the ache in his back. Careful not to twist, he did his best to stretch the sore muscles and decided walking a few minutes more could only help. Propping one foot up on the nearby fence, he gazed at the horizon laid out before him. It had been one hell of a long time since he'd seen so much of nothing in one place. Focusing on the clear sky as blue as a child's crayon, he forced himself to think of childhood drawings, the bright blue dress his date wore on prom night—the one he'd worked so hard to talk her out of—and the twinkle in his grandmother's slate blue eyes while she sang an Irish limerick. Anything not to think of the similarities to the dry, flat and hotter than Hades sandbox.

Some days the Marine Corps seemed so far away, so long ago. Other days, the years spent someplace nobody wanted him to be, certainly not the natives, seemed too close for comfort. Now back in the civilized world—and on occasion he questioned exactly what about modern day urban life constituted civility—hanging onto hope for a better world seemed an awfully damn hard thing to do.

Screwing the cap back on the water, he gave himself a mental kick. Wallowing in his own dang thoughts wasn't going to make things any better either. Things were what they were. Returning the bottle to his backpack, he took one lingering look at the vastness before him. Time to get moving. Swinging his leg over the seat with a little more agility than when he'd climbed off the new motorcycle, he knocked up the kickstand and started the engine.

Spitting bits of roadside dirt and gravel, the tires gripped the asphalt road. Ready to push every single horsepower to its limits, he leaned forward and that sixth sense that more than once had saved his life pushed him to glance quickly across the road. His heart and his motorcycle skidded to a sudden stop.

The last thing he'd expected to see in the middle of Damn Nowhere West Texas was a horse up on its hind legs, front feet kicking, and a petite beauty sliding off its back—crashing hard on the unforgiving dirt. Flashes of heavy hooves with a thousand pounds of momentum coming down on her was all it took for him to spin around and race across the road. Both in the sandbox and the civilized world, he'd had enough of needless death to last him a lifetime. Enough was enough.

CHAPTER TWO

"Whoa." Hannah gripped the reins, pulling tightly on the horse. "Whoa girl," she repeated, but there was no calming the animal down. She knew from the second Starburst's ears twitched that she might be in trouble. The sound of the rider back on his bike, kicking the engine into gear and roaring to life from across the road had put the mare on high—and nervous--alert. It was Hannah's own fault really. At first when she'd seen the driver stopped in the distance, she'd taken too long to debate whether to hightail it out of there or go find out if the stranger needed help. Sometimes cell phones didn't cooperate out here.

In this neck of the woods stranded riders on motorcycles were not the most common thing in the world. On the other hand, strangers passing through did happen, so anything was possible. After all, West Texas wasn't exactly outer space.

But before she'd had a chance to process moving forward with this new horse, the stranger had seen fit to rev the engine, scaring the living hell out of her mount. If that wasn't enough he'd done it twice more before taking off like the hounds of hell were on his heels. The overused cliché from one too many romance books fit the situation all too well.

Next thing she knew, Hannah found herself on a very agitated horse. Leaning over the saddle horn, preparing to sweet talk the nervous equine, she'd been caught totally off guard as the mare's hind legs went up high and landed hard. Hannah might as well have been on a busting bronc at the rodeo. There was no time to shift her weight or soothe the horse. With a quick jerk, the animal's forelegs came up off the ground one more time, breaking her grip free of the reins. Staring up at the clear blue sky, she went flying through the air. It all happened so fast, she'd had no time to exhale or mentally prepare. The animal had thrown her as easily as a tempestuous child could throw a rag doll. Only rag dolls couldn't break.

"Miss," a muddled voice whispered. "Don't move."

Move? At this point her eyelids seemed too heavy to lift, never mind an arm or leg. Sucking in a slow almost gasping breath, Hannah managed to open one eye and then the other. Sunlight made her want to clamp the lids shut once again, but instead, squinting, she turned her head toward the voice.

"Please try not to move. Does anything hurt?"

"You mean besides breathing?"

Worried eyes twinkled down at her with a hint of amusement. "Yes. Besides breathing."

She moved her fingers and wiggled her toes. Shifting her arms, she pushed up on her elbows.

"Whoa. I don't think it's a good idea you move just yet."

How the heck was she supposed to know if anything hurt if she didn't move? "I just got the wind knocked out of me." And rubbing her hand to a tender spot behind her ear, she suspected she was going to have one hell of a knot.

"You hit your head, didn't you?" That serious look of concern took over the stranger's face again.

"Amongst other things."

"I'll give you extra points for a sense of humor. But if you don't mind, I'd like to check for broken bones."

She wasn't sure if he expected her to agree or argue, but the minor attempt at bobbing her head sent a shooting pain up her neck to the burgeoning knot. "Mm hmm," she muttered instead.

Strong hands carefully swiped from her shoulders down each arm, and then from hip to ankle. The way he held her foot and tenderly turned it left then right, she had the distinct feeling this was not the first time he'd been in a situation like this. Not that he had made a habit of knocking women off their horses, but she guessed he had some experience in first aid. As a matter fact, the way gentle fingers maneuvered across the bone much like a concert pianist making love to the ivory keys, she wouldn't be surprised to learn he was a doctor.

"Nothing seems broken, but the EMTs will probably want to get you on a backboard before taking you to the hospital."

EMTs? Did this guy have a clue where they were? Despite his concerns, Hannah pushed herself upright.

"I really wish you wouldn't do that." The stranger put his phone to his ear.

"If it's 911 you're calling, at this time of day you're going to get Esther at the station, she's going to call my cousin Brooks, and he's going to ask me how do I feel. I'll tell him *fine*, just had the wind knocked out of me, and he'll come over for dinner to make sure. Or, we could do this the easy way."

Phone still at his ear, his brows dipped. "How's that?"

"You let me get up. Let me get on the horse. Then wait for me to ride away before turning that horse-spooking Honda back on."

"It's a Harley. I'm sorry about the horse, but I'd still like you to stay put until a professional sees you."

Now that she was sitting upright and breathing easier, she took a moment to look at the leather-clad stranger. Not exactly a suit of armor, though he certainly had a streak of male chivalry suitable for a knight rescuing a damsel in distress. That was, if she were in distress. "I'm fine. If it makes you feel any better I promise to call my cousin myself and let him know what happened as soon as I get home."

The stranger pulled the phone away from his ear and stared down at it. "Doesn't look like I'm going to reach anyone this way." He dropped it into a breast pocket and looked around as though wishing a car to amble by.

"You are stubborn, aren't you?"

A shock of surprise flashed across his face. "Let's just say this isn't sitting well with me."

None of this was sitting all that well with her either. "Okay." She shoved her hands down on the ground and pushed upright.

"Enough is enough." No sooner had she straightened than the ground shifted beneath her.

"Whoa." Stretching forward, strong hands gently grabbed her arms. "See? And unfortunately, putting you on the back of the bike isn't going to be any better than you riding that horse off into the sunset. How far are we from town?"

"You mean the way the crow flies?"

"That far?" He ran one hand roughly across the back of his neck.

She dared a nod, relieved the knot at the back of her head hadn't objected, and the ground beneath her saw fit to remain stable. "Yes, and you can let go of me now. The world has stopped spinning."

By now Starburst had made her way over and was gently sniffing at Hannah's shoulder. "Sorry, girl. Didn't mean to scare you."

"Scare *her*?" The stranger's eyes rounded.

Hannah scratched under Starburst's jaw and took in the animal's unexpectedly calm demeanor. "Maybe you'll work out after all," she cooed, "as long as we keep you away from two-wheelers." She lifted her gaze to meet both the cause of her current dilemma as well as her rescuer. "I promise I will be fine but I do need to head back or people are going to start to wonder if I decided to ride all the way to Dallas."

"If you insist on riding home, I'll follow you." The way he looked from her to the saddle and back with such concern in his eyes, she couldn't very well say no.

"Fine." Moving in front of the saddle she lifted one foot into the stirrup, grabbed hold of the saddle horn, and just as she started to pull up stars danced in front of the horizon. Prepared to land once again flat on her back, instead she found herself cradled in the stranger's arms.

His dark eyes were heavy with concern. "I'm still not so sure about this idea of yours."

To tell the truth she was starting to have some doubts herself, but there weren't a whole lot of choices because she sure as hell wasn't going to get on the backend of that motorcycle, nor was she willing to leave Starburst standing in the field by herself. The only choice she had was to pull up her big girl panties and get herself home, but first she'd have to extricate herself from this man's arms and prove she could stand on her own two feet. "You can put me down now."

Of all the possible thoughts crossing his mind, cooperation didn't appear to be one of them. For just a moment or two she thought he might actually refuse and simply carry her all the way home. Another long pause hung between them before he slid one hand out from under her, letting her feet touch the ground, then cautiously eased the other hand away as well. Taking in a deep breath, she stuck her foot in the stirrup to climb up again, only this time his hands were at her side just in case.

Swinging her leg over, she straightened in the seat and blew out a grateful breath, relieved to be perfectly balanced. "Better give me a head start. I don't need Starburst spooking again. When I'm almost out of your sight it'll probably be safe for you to start that contraption up. Agreed?"

Another moment of hesitation passed but he had to be as aware as she was that they had little other choice. "Agreed."

Grabbing hold of the reins she tugged left, turning Starburst in the direction of the ranch. The unexpected and almost absurd encounter had her glancing around looking for any sign of a mysterious dog. Nothing in sight. *Too bad.* Would've made one hell of a story to tell her grandchildren.

• • • •

There wasn't a single thing about the unfolding scenario that rubbed Dale the right way. He felt terrible if it had indeed been his motorcycle that spooked the horse, but he couldn't help but think horses shouldn't spook that easily. Then again, what made him an expert on horses?

Waiting longer than he would have liked, and not nearly as long as he probably should have, he knocked the kickstand up and gave the engine a start. The Harley beneath him roared to life. Maybe he really should've just gone east on I-20. Keeping her figure ahead in his sights, he shook his head. *Or not.*

Riding slower than he'd ever gone on a motorcycle in his entire life, including when he learned how to ride one in the first place, he followed behind the young lady at a safe distance. More than once he'd been tempted to inch up a little closer, but fear of watching her fly off the horse again kept his impatience at bay. Sort of.

The fence along the side of the road shifted to whitewashed wood that blended easily into a large stone wall under an impressive metal archway. *Capaill.* Most likely the tiny house in the distance wouldn't be so tiny once they pulled up closer. If he remained by the gate he could see that she made it inside. The fewer people he dealt with the better, but there was no way he could drive off without seeing that she was safe. And personally, handing her to... Who? He hadn't even gotten her name. Didn't know if she lived alone, with a husband, with her parents, or the doctor cousin that she promised to call.

Once she'd stepped onto the front porch, he picked up speed to arrive more quickly, but not so fast as to spook the horse again. Just because she was no longer in the saddle didn't mean that he wanted to upset the animal. He was nearly to the front of the house before cutting the engine and walking the rest of the way in.

The gal had spunk. Arms crossed and toe tapping, she greeted him. "As you can see I made it home just fine."

The front door opened wide behind her and a tall dark-haired man with an air of familiarity stood filling the doorway. "We were starting to wonder if we should send out a search party." The man's eyes drifted to the bike and then back to the woman. "I see you've made a friend."

"Yes. Connor, this is..." Her words trailed off as she pointed at him. "So much for southern hospitality. I don't even know your name."

"Da...vid at your service, ma'am." The fake name was improvisation, but the polite exchange left him with an inexplicable urge to click his heels and bow at the waist. How stupid would that have looked?

Arm extended, his damsel in distress smiled. "Nice to meet you, David. I'm Hannah."

"Connor Farraday." In turn, the man on the porch extended his hand.

Farraday? So he'd reached Farraday country. Of course. The doctor cousin—Brooks. Now it all made sense. "You may want to have a doctor take a quick look. She fell off her horse."

"You what?" Connor's head whipped around in Hannah's direction, his alarmed gaze scanned her quickly from top to toe.

"This isn't the first, nor will it be the last time my derrière has hit the ground."

Connor turned to face him. "She does have a point. But look at us standing here on the porch like a couple of city folk. Please come in. I'll get my wife."

Dale wasn't in a hurry exactly, so there was no reason to object, but somehow he felt this wasn't his decision. Meeting Hannah's gaze, he waited a second for her to nod slowly before raising her hand to the back of her neck.

"Let me see." Without waiting for approval, he took a step closer and stretching out his arm, placed his hand beside hers, gently touching the affected area. "You've got a nice bump there. Better get some ice for that while we wait for the doctor."

"Doctor?" An attractive redhead now stood in the doorway where Connor had been moments before. "Are you okay?"

Hannah rolled her eyes and blew out an exasperated breath. "Oh brother. It's just a bump on the head."

Panic quickly filled the redhead's eyes. "Head? Connor's on the phone with Brooks. I suspect he'll be here very quickly. In the meantime we'd better get you inside and off your feet." As an afterthought, she turned and looked at him over her shoulder. "Are you hurt too?"

"No, ma'am. You might say I'm the reason she fell off her horse."

Confusion mangled with distrust stared back at him.

"What he means is," Hannah drew the redhead's attention away from him, "the sound of his motorcycle spooked Starburst. She bucked like a bronc and sent me flying."

"I see," she said cautiously. "And it's Catherine, not ma'am." A curly haired little girl came running up to them, stopping short at the sofa. Her inquisitive little gaze transferred from the redhead to Hannah to him and back. "Are you sick, Aunt Hannah?"

Smart kid.

"No, sweetie. I'm just fine."

He noticed she failed to mention falling off the horse, and the redhead didn't add to it.

"Is Starburst okay?" the little girl asked.

"Yes, she is. But I bet she'd like a treat from her favorite girl."

The little girl beamed up at them, nodded, and spun about, running in the direction she'd come from, calling out, "Daddy, I need a carrot for Starburst."

"Hold up there." Connor nearly collided with the child. "She's out front still. Get a carrot from the fridge and take it to her. I'll be out soon and we'll take her back to the barn and clean her up."

Still grinning, the little girl nodded and rushed past her father into what he could only guess was the kitchen. Hannah dropped gingerly onto the sofa, the muffled sound of movement drifted in from the kitchen and before anyone moved, the little girl came rushing back in, waving a carrot, and hurried out the front door without a word.

The redhead winced as the little girl slammed the door shut behind her and turned to Connor. "Do you think there will ever be a day when I'm not worried about Stacey and the horses?"

"Deep down," Connor smiled at his wife, "we all worry just a tiny bit about everything our children do out of our sight."

The redhead smiled back at him. "I suppose you're right. Soon it'll be boys then cars that make me nervous."

"You mean cars, then college, then work, then boys. Because we all know she's not dating till she's thirty five," Connor deadpanned.

The words may have been said as a joke, but Dale knew deep down, there was probably more truth than jest in the father's statement.

"Did you get a hold of Brooks?" Catherine asked.

"He and Toni are actually already on their way to the ranch to pick up some pans Toni needs to borrow from Aunt Eileen. Apparently she's in baking overload. He'll be stopping here first."

"Ah, nesting," Connor's wife confirmed.

"Yeah, well, soon Brooks will tell you I'm just fine and everything can get back to normal around here." Lifting her hand halfway to the knot on her head, Hannah seemed to think better and dropped her arm to her side.

"It might be a good idea to give her a bag of ice for that bump she's got. My guess is it's going to be a real goose egg, which is way better than a hematoma, but she might want a couple of aspirins to go with the ice pack."

"I'll get it." The redhead turned to face him. "I'm sorry, where are my manners? Can I get you something to drink while I'm in the kitchen?"

"No, thank you, ma'am. Just passing through. I won't be here that long." There was at least one thing he was sure of—it was in everyone's best interest for him to keep moving.

CHAPTER THREE

"It'll take a lot more than a bump on the head to take down a Farraday." Brooks Farraday stuffed his stethoscope into his bag.

"Told ya." Hannah flashed her cousin a toothy grin. The way this family was fussing about, you'd think she'd never been around a horse in her life. Every single member of the Farraday clan had fallen off a horse more times than they could count on both their hands and feet. Well maybe at least both their hands. Why they were making such a fuss now she had no idea.

"At least you can give her a ride back to the ranch." Catherine shifted her attention from Brooks to the guest still in the living room. "And I'm sure Aunt Eileen will want to thank you for watching out for Hannah. It's getting close to supper and she's probably cooked enough for an army."

"I'd say more than just the Army. Throw in the Navy and the Marine Corps too." Normally Hannah would've been just as glad to get rid of this guy. Put the whole incident behind her. Certainly not give her aunt any more excuses to worry about her. But for some reason, Hannah liked the idea of getting to know a little bit more about this stranger besides his first name.

Now that she had a chance to sit and look him over, she realized she must have been hit harder in the head than she'd thought. That was the only possible explanation for not spotting those twinkling caramel eyes right off the bat. Not to mention the guy was built like a man who knew his way around hard work. Or a gym. Or perhaps both.

"Absolutely." Toni sat beside Hannah, waiting with baited breath for her husband's conclusions. "Aunt Eileen will be annoyed with all of us if we let you get away without at least feeding you."

"That won't be necessary." David briefly flashed a tired smile.

Hannah hadn't given it any thought, but he'd probably ridden a long while, which would explain why he'd been standing by the side of the road. Finding her sprawled out in the middle of the field probably had taken its toll on him as well. "Have you got a place to stay tonight? We have plenty of guest rooms."

The varied reactions in the room to her suggestion almost made her laugh. Toni patted her leg as though it had been a brilliant idea. Catherine cast a glance at the stranger again and gave an almost unnoticeable shrug. Brooks on the other hand looked like an owl with his claw stuck in an electric socket. She wasn't sure if David noticed or not, but she thought she saw the corner of his lip twitch with the hint of amusement.

"That's very thoughtful of you, but there's no need. I'm heading to a bed and breakfast in Tuckers Bluff that looks like a good spot to bunk for the night."

"Meg's place," Catherine said enthusiastically.

"Meg?"

"She's married to my cousin Adam." Hannah pushed to her feet. "I say we debate this over supper. I'm hungry, I'm tired, and did I mention I'm hungry?"

Brooks shook his head. "Tell us something we don't already know. Are you ever not hungry?"

This time David definitely smiled. A killer smile. "I should really," his words caught as he stood from the old recliner, rubbing his thigh and grimacing, "be on my way."

Frowning, Brooks moved toward him. "Cramps?"

"No. Just stiff."

"How long were you on the bike?"

David straightened into his full height and pressing his lips tightly together, stretched his back before retreating a step. "Not long. A couple of hours. Maybe three. Maybe more."

"More?" Brooks' gaze narrowed, focusing more intently on

the man in front of him. "Where'd you come from?"

"East."

The crevice in Brooks' forehead deepened. "I see."

Hannah had to agree with what she knew was running through her cousin's mind. East was an awfully vague answer. Especially since more than half the country was east of West Texas. "Sounds like a walk to stretch your legs and loosen your back would do you some good. If you join us for supper, maybe the doc here can give you some exercises to help ease the discomfort."

"You probably know just as much about that as I do." Brooks flashed her a bright smile.

David's hands fell quickly to his sides. "You a physical therapist?"

"Not even close. Equine assisted therapist. As a matter of fact, if the doctor says it's okay, and you're sticking around a while, a little time on the horse could help strengthen your back."

David shook his head. "Just a little stiff. Besides, that kind of therapy would take a lot more time than I have to spare." Almost as if trying to soften the blow of the rejection, he flashed her a bright grin.

"You can leave the motorcycle here," Catherine offered. "It will be more comfortable riding over to the ranch in the Suburban."

"That won't be—"

"Bike will be waiting here after dinner. By then you should be up to the ride into town." Catherine turned to the rest of the family. "All right, let's get moving. Now we're all hungry." She waved her arms, encouraging everybody to move forward. Without an argument from anyone, the adults fell into a single file line out the door.

Falling in line behind Catherine, Hannah leaned into her in-law's side, lowering her voice. "You handled that just like Aunt Eileen."

Catherine beamed at her, a slow steady smile spreading across her face. "I did, didn't I?"

"Yeah, you did." Following their guest to Brooks' Suburban, Hannah swallowed a smile of her own. Life in West Texas Farraday country sure was turning out to be a hell of a lot more interesting than she'd ever imagined.

• • • •

In only a few hours the picture of the Farraday family had become very clear in Dale's mind. He couldn't have been in the house more than fifteen minutes before Aunt Eileen had him relaxed on a recliner with a heating pad behind his back. Once assured that Dale wasn't on any additional medication, she'd insisted he have one beer. Thirty minutes later she had him up walking around the room stretching before letting him sit back down with the heating pad again. His brief stint at the hospital hadn't come close to the care this woman was giving him.

"Would you like another beer?" she asked.

"No, ma'am. One's my limit on the bike."

Aunt Eileen beamed at him as though he were a teenager who had just given his mother the right answer. He couldn't help but return the smile. The entire meal, the banter, the teasing, the camaraderie had explained so much. And the pretty brunette across the table from him was doing more good to his tired soul than the heating pad, the beer, or the family love bouncing off the walls.

Hannah pushed back out of her chair and picked up both their plates. "Would you like some ice cream with your pie?"

He was all set to decline dessert when he remembered somebody had used the words fresh-baked midway through dinner. He wasn't sure he'd ever had a homemade blueberry pie, and wasn't about to pass up the chance for a first time now. Though he had a feeling if he stuck around much longer, there'd be a lot more firsts in store for him. "Plain is fine. Thank you."

The very pregnant woman at his other side leaned in conspiratorially. "Ice cream is homemade too. You may want to try it. Just saying." Nestled back upright, resting her hands on her well-rounded stomach, she winked at him.

"Sounds good," he agreed. "Thank you."

"We Yankees have to stick together."

With more out of state residents than Texans living in the Dallas suburbs, he wasn't used to being called out as a Yankee, but was rather pleased with the newfound kinship.

"Where are you from?" Toni asked.

"Born in upstate New York. Philadelphia for high school, and just about any place Uncle Sam sent me after that before settling in Texas."

"In the military?"

"Marine."

"Ah, a jarhead."

He gave her a big smile despite the needling nickname. The lady was just too cute to be irritated with.

"Don't look at me like that." Toni rolled her eyes at him like an older sister silently putting her baby brother in his place. And wasn't that just a hoot. "I have three brothers-in-law, two of them former Marines, one of them a helicopter pilot soon to be added to the ranks of former Marine."

He shook his head at her, but continued smiling. "You know what they say—"

"I didn't say ex-Marine," she cut him off, "I said former."

Connor came walking up to the table with two dishes in hand. "Once a Marine—"

"—Always a Marine," both men echoed.

Toni rolled her eyes again and muttered, "Men."

The pie was well worth the delay and probably on his new list of favorites. "This is amazing." He waved a fork at the aunt.

"Glad you like it. You're welcome back for more any time you're in the area."

"Thank you." Maybe, someday, if he got his future back, he could take her up on the offer. By the time he'd polished off the pie and the ice cream and the cup of coffee Aunt Eileen insisted he have, another hour had passed. "Thank you so much for your hospitality, but it's time I hit the road."

"Listen, man," Connor came up beside him, "it's a bit of a ways into town and a ride on that bike has got to be tough after a long day. Why don't we toss it in the back of the truck and give you a lift into town?"

The cowboy looked at him, his expression blank, his gaze steady.

If Dale had to make a flash decision, he'd say the offer wasn't simply expected politeness but sincere. "Thanks, but that won't be necessary."

"Correct. It isn't necessary, but I'm offering nonetheless." Connor hadn't come right out and said as much, but the implication, the reminder of Semper Fi, was clear.

"Appreciated, but it's best I just get on my way. Thank you for the hospitality." He turned to Hannah. "And I'm glad to see you're feeling fine. I really am sorry about the horse."

"All in a day's work." She smiled up at him. "All in a day's work."

Aunt Eileen stood in front of him, her hands on her hips, her sweet smile clearly meant to disarm the most stubborn. "I cannot think of a single good reason not to accept Connor's offer of a lift into town. There's no weakness in admitting you're hurting."

The way the last words rolled off her tongue, Dale had the distinct feeling she was talking about much more than his injured back. Added to the small snickers and smiles spreading across the faces of the few people still at the table and Dale wasn't at all sure how to respond besides a simple, "Thank you, Miss Eileen."

"It's *Aunt* Eileen. There's no miss around here."

"Excuse me. Thank you, Aunt Eileen. But honestly, I'm fine to drive. Really. You've taken excellent care of me. Probably better care than I've had, well, in a long time. I'll be fine, I promise."

Easing her stance, her hands fell by her side and she nodded. The glimmer of acceptance in her eyes made him feel marginally better. A small part of him wanted to take them up on the easier ride. Another small part wanted to join this crazy familial world that he had now become even more at home with over the course of one single dinner.

But this was not his world, and there was no way he would bring his world down on these nice people. Not now. Not ever.

CHAPTER FOUR

Dale saw the lights of the small town ahead. From what he already knew, Tuckers Bluff was one of those one stoplight towns, but not until actually riding down Main Street, passing the café, the small shops, the town square, did he realize exactly how small was *small*. Up ahead he saw the lit sign for the lone police station and decided now was as good a time as any to deal with the reason he'd chosen to ride through Tuckers Bluff. Pulling his bike into a space in front and setting down the kickstand, he slid off the bike, straightened to his full height and unstrapped his helmet. Taking longer than he needed to settle his headgear onto the motorcycle, he steeled himself for the next bridge to cross.

Even though it was against standard procedure, he couldn't go through with the plan without setting at least one person straight. Opening the door and stepping inside the country office, he looked left and spotted the dispatcher at her desk. A middle-aged woman on the phone repeating "Yes, ma'am, I understand," and a few "I know it's not easy," she looked up at him, smiled, and lifted a finger. "Yes, ma'am. I'll see to it that someone comes by and takes a look right away. I'm sure it will be fine. See you on Sunday." She stood and met his questioning gaze head on. "What can I do for you?"

"I'd like to speak with the police chief."

The dispatcher sized him up from head to toe and then from toe to head. "Police chief Farraday is out of the office at the moment. Perhaps I can—"

"No, ma'am. I'd rather wait for the chief."

Her steely gaze sharpened. "It may be a while before the chief is back in the office. If this is an emergency…" She let the words hang.

"No, ma'am. Not an emergency. A courtesy. I'm staying at the bed and breakfast in town. I will stop by after I've checked in. Perhaps I can catch him then."

"Shall I give him a message?"

"No, ma'am. As I said. Just a courtesy call."

The officer looked at him long and hard. Finally she offered a brief nod of her head and retook her seat. With a return nod, he pivoted around and marched out the front door. If he read her face right, and he was pretty sure he could read this one, the second the door slammed shut behind him, she would be on the phone to DJ telling him there was a stranger in town looking for him. Dale liked the look of her face. He had the feeling that if all hell broke loose, she was one of the officers that could be trusted to have your back. For a small-town police force, DJ probably put together one of the best in Texas.

• • • •

"Well that was a nice young man." Aunt Eileen stood at the sink loading the dishwasher. "And he just rode up and spooked the horse, knocking you out of the saddle?"

"Yep, that pretty much covers it." Hannah wiped the counter down.

"And you're sure there wasn't anything else around to have spooked the horse?"

Hannah rolled her eyes. This was the third time Aunt Eileen had asked her about something else in the vicinity. The woman was poking for the mystery dog. Apparently her aunt's matchmaking radar was on high alert and only the absence of a shaggy dog was preventing her from hogtying the stranger and dragging him back to the house until he proposed. "Sorry, Aunt Eileen. No dog on the road, no dog in the fields, no dog in the shadows. No dog."

Her aunt nodded. "Well, he does seem a bit broken."

Hannah bit back a groan. She wasn't sure if her aunt was referring to the back or something inside the man. Not that it mattered. She'd seen that isolated look in his eyes in too many people. There was definitely something that was hurting and she felt sure his back wasn't the half of it. Then again, most people had something at some point in their lives that hurt them deep inside. The people we love the most can do the worst damage. Life was a cycle. Death, love, joy, pain, so many different things contributing to who we are. Whatever the pieces of the puzzle were that had made their dinner guest the man he was, she'd admit, at least to herself, this guy definitely intrigued her.

"Are you two still talking about that dog?" Her uncle Sean came up behind her and kissed her on the cheek then shook his head at his sister-in-law. "Sometimes, Eileen, I wonder when you got bit by this silly notion that every single person within Tuckers Bluff city limits should be married."

Aunt Eileen wiped her hands on the dish rag and tossed it on the countertop, then turned to face her brother in law. "Every single person in town? Really?" She shook her head, smiling. "Heaven knows nobody would want to marry off the sisters. Not to mention all the young ones who need time to grow up. But if there's a good match I certainly wouldn't want somebody to miss out on it. Look how happy your children are. When it's right, it's right. That's all I'm saying." She leaned forward and kissed Hannah on the cheek. "I'm off to bed early to curl up with a good book."

That sounded like an excellent idea. Hannah had bought a book not too long ago in town thinking that curling up with an old-fashioned paperback could be a nice reprieve from the last-minute stresses of the upcoming riding programs. Except she hadn't had a single moment to herself where she wasn't too tired to hold the thing in her hands. Tonight was going to be the night. "I'm going to call it an early night too."

Her uncle Sean followed behind a few steps before snapping his fingers. "I almost forgot." He turned and headed back toward his office, returning a few seconds later with an envelope in hand. "This was slipped inside my *Texas Monthly* magazine. Meant to give it to you earlier today."

"Thanks." Eyes nearly crossed, Eileen studied the return address and if Hannah wasn't mistaken, paled a shade or two.

"Bad news?" Sean Farraday inched closer.

So Hannah wasn't the only one who thought her aunt's reaction to the envelope hadn't been a good thing.

Aunt Eileen shook her head, lifted her chin, and slipped the envelope into her pocket. "No. Probably junk mail. You'd think by now advertisers would learn people don't read snail mail and stop sending us all this crap."

Uncle Sean hesitated before smiling, satisfied with the explanation. "I think the post office needs it to stay in business."

Aunt Eileen returned the smile. "Sleep well." Her hand in her pocket, she headed up the stairs.

Hannah followed on her heels to the door of her cousin Adam's old room. For Hannah, it felt the same as being home. As young girls, she and her cousin Grace had spent many a night giggling and laughing and tormenting the older boys, hiding under the bed, in the closet and anywhere else where they might play tricks. Together, they'd laughed and joked, they'd teased, they'd tumbled and practiced somersaults and hand stands. And of course, like all giddy young girls, shared secrets from their diaries. Yep, just like home.

Another round of *good night* and *sleep well* crossed between her aunt, her uncle and herself as each one entered their room and closed the doors behind them. Watching her aunt and uncle was like watching her mom and dad. Though much about the relationship made no sense. Hannah's cousins had been long grown, and yet Aunt Eileen was still as much a staple at this household as Uncle Sean.

Once the kids had started moving away, if it had been Hannah, she would have been looking for her own match, or maybe someone for Uncle Sean. Then again, what the hell did she know about raising children and growing old. She had her hands full just understanding horses and struggling students. Some questions in life simply weren't meant to be answered.

Opening the anticipated novel, she read the first few lines. The hero was tall and handsome with dark hair, dark eyes, and of course the requisite chiseled features, strong arms, tight shirt. No matter how hard she tried to make a different image come to mind, every time the hero came on the scene, David popped into her mind. Maybe reading a book hadn't been the best idea she had.

• • • •

"Esther, slow down." DJ had already been on his way back to the station when his dispatcher had reached out to him, huffing about a stranger in town. That was not like Esther. Of all the people in his office she was usually the one who could keep the calm in the chaos. "What exactly did he say?"

"I told you that three times already. He said '*It's just a courtesy call.*' I had my share of courtesy calls and they're usually preceded by '*I am officer so and so, from whatever city, and I'm here to report to the police chief, whatever.*'" Under her breath she muttered, 'Courtesy call my ass.' "I'm telling you, this guy has something to hide. I don't know who he is, or what he is, but he's staying at your sister-in-law's bed and breakfast. And I, for one, think it would behoove you to get your backside over there sooner rather than later."

The sense of urgency in Esther's voice hadn't eased up as she repeated the same information. He wasn't sure about this one. His cop gut was keeping suspiciously quiet, but he trusted Esther's gut. With his life if he had to. And especially with his sister-in-law's life. "What about Reed? How far away is he?"

"Now you're thinking like a cop. And of course if he'd been closer, I'd have sent him. He's not. The job is yours. So get moving."

For a split second, DJ felt he was the subordinate and Esther his superior. But he did as he was told. His father and aunt hadn't raised any fools. "On my way."

Not ready to turn on the lights and sirens to fly through town for no darn good reason, he was perfectly willing to hit the gas pedal and perhaps bend a few minor speeding laws. Careful not to become a road hazard, he made it to Meg's place considerably faster than he might have on a regular evening drive. Pulling into the driveway, he noticed the motorcycle parked by the curb wheels out. He checked the plates, taking note for later. Just in case.

Especially aware of every inch of the surroundings as he approached the house, looking for any sign of something even slightly off thanks to the stranger in town, DJ hadn't expected to reach the front door and hear the sound of laughter. Not till he blew out a relieved breath did he realize how much he'd come to trust Esther's instincts. To the best of his memory Esther had never been one to overreact but, thankfully, that appeared to be just the case. This time.

Opening the door DJ followed the amused voices to the kitchen. Meg stood by the sink, a tea kettle in hand, laughing so hard tears rolled down her cheeks. Adam stood off to the side holding a couple of coffee mugs that he'd pulled from the cupboard, a rumble from deep in his chest matched his wife's. No wonder the sound of laughter had carried down the hall and through the front door. Seated at the large center island, his back to DJ, Esther's stranger chuckled along with the others.

DJ wasn't all that sure who was telling the stories but he was willing to bet it was the guy whose face he'd yet to see. "Sounds like everybody's having a good time without me." He approached the island.

"David here has been telling corny jokes." Meg poured water into the two cups that Adam had set before her.

Curious to see the guy's face, DJ got a little closer. Before he could casually ease around for a better look, the man stood and turned, extending his hand to him. "I'm David Brubaker. How do you do?"

DJ stood dumbfounded. David Brubaker? The guy held a straight face, looked him dead in the eye, didn't blink, didn't flinch. None of it made sense. DJ accepted the proffered hand. "Nice to meet you."

"David is just passing through." Meg filled her own cup with hot water. "Wouldn't mind if he were staying a few days. I'd love to have a repertoire of good jokes to share with the guests. It's so hard to find cute clean jokes nowadays."

"I'll be glad to leave a few written down before I go," David said with a smile. "My grandfather loved telling stories. It's fun to share them. Almost like having Grandpa here again."

"Oh that's so nice," Meg practically cooed before lifting up the coffee pot in DJ's direction. "Would you like some tea or coffee, DJ?"

He'd just finished a supersized cup of coffee before the call had come in from Esther, but he'd look pretty silly stopping by at this hour for no good reason. "Just what I needed. Thank you very much." He pulled up a stool next to the stranger. Right height. Right build. Right face—wrong name.

CHAPTER FIVE

The second that Meg and Adam disappeared from the kitchen, Dale knew he was in for a lot of explaining.

Sure enough, DJ looked him straight in the face. "Want to tell me what the hell is going on?"

"That's why I'm here."

Meg walked back into the room. "I forgot to take the cinnamon rolls out of the freezer. I have to put them in the oven first thing in the morning, and it never works the same if I bake them frozen."

The two men tracked the gracious redhead as she crossed the room and retrieved the pan from the commercial grade freezer, set the frozen rolls on the counter, and then smiling, waved to them on her way out of the room again. "If you need anything don't hesitate to ask. Like I said, Adam and I are up on the third floor."

"I'll be fine, thank you. The room looks very comfortable and you've given me everything I could need and more."

Meg nodded and both men waited until the sound of her heels clacking disappeared up the stairs.

DJ shifted in his seat. "Start talking."

"I wanted you to see for yourself that I'm okay. Cap told me you've been keeping tabs on me at the hospital."

"I have. You're looking awfully good for a guy who not very long ago was touch and go."

"Yeah, that's the whole thing." Now that he stood in front of DJ, Dale had second thoughts about how much he should tell the best partner he'd ever had about what put him in the hospital in the first place and why he was riding clear to New Mexico via every back road in the state of Texas.

DJ didn't let the silence linger. "I'm sure you didn't drive all this way just to tell me you're fine and not tell me anything else."

"Actually, that's exactly what I did." He needed to say more. "But no one can know I was here."

Shaking his head, DJ pushed the half-empty tea cup further away. "How bad is it?"

"Under control." He hoped.

DJ stared long and hard at him. "You're not supposed to be here."

Dale shook his head. If anyone knew he detoured through Tuckers Bluff to reach out to DJ, it would be more than his life on the line. It could be DJ's. "No. That's why I'm only here for tonight and then I'm moving on. But I needed you to know for yourself no matter what you hear, this is my reality."

Gaze narrowing and the muscles along his jaw clenching, DJ eyed his friend. Odds were every cop instinct DJ had were drawing conclusions pretty damn close to the truth. But DJ was a good enough cop to know that he was better off guessing and not confirming. His head bobbed once. "Okay. We'll do this your way. For now."

"Thanks." Relieved, Dale reached for his coffee.

"About the accident—"

"It's not what you think." Dale shook his head.

"How do you know what I think?"

"You're worried that murder suicide call was too much for me. The final straw."

"Was it?" DJ's expression remained stoic, but his eyes did a lousy job of hiding his concern.

Best partner *and* friend Dale ever had. He sucked in a long breath. That miserable night was damn near close to the last straw. He'd done a good job of wallowing in a few drinks after his shift. Civilized world his ass. "I won't BS you. Close. We've seen too much." When all this was over, if it ever ended, it might be a good time for a change.

The slightest dip of DJ's chin, showed he understood exactly how Dale felt.

The rest of what was going on in Dale's life was better left unsaid. "There's one thing you need to know. On my way here I had a little run in with your cousin Hannah."

"Run in?"

"Yeah. My motorcycle spooked the horse she was riding and knocked her on the ground."

Alarm flashed strong and hard in DJ's eyes.

"She's fine," Dale said hurriedly. He probably should've said that first. "But she did take me back with her to Connor's house. I couldn't just let her ride off with a bump on the head. I wanted to make sure she was okay. Brooks checked her over and confirmed she is indeed fine. Then your Aunt Eileen insisted on feeding me. I couldn't get out of it."

Tension eased from DJ's face momentarily as a smile teased his lips. "That's not a surprise."

"Yeah. Since dinner, things make a lot more sense to me."

This time DJ laughed outright. "I bet."

"It shouldn't mean anything. And there shouldn't be a problem. Or I wouldn't have stayed."

"I know that."

"But just in case, you need to know. I was there."

"Got it. Are you sure this is the way you want to handle it?"

If DJ had asked him that five hours ago Dale would've answered with an emphatic yes. But now, he just wasn't so sure.

• • • •

While the rest of the ranch was in the habit of waking before sunup to beat the midday Texas heat, Hannah's routine didn't start until something more akin to business hours. Except for this morning. Eyes wide open in the pitch of black, she gave up on sleep, and decided simply starting her day at the crack of dawn made more sense.

"You're up awfully early this morning." Aunt Eileen stood over the stove poking at a frying pan.

"I'm anxious to get more time in with the new horses." While the statement was the truth, she'd left out it wasn't only the horses that kept her mind working overtime. Something about yesterday's visitor poked at her much the way her aunt was stabbing at the bacon in the frying pan. She couldn't quite put her finger on why she just couldn't let go of the stranger. "How can I help?"

"The boys will be back and sitting down any minute. I'm running just a little behind. Why don't you set the table for me and grab a couple of containers of orange juice from the fridge?"

"Will do."

By the time Finn and her uncle Sean had joined them at the table a hint of daylight peeked through the kitchen window. She was itching to work some more with Starburst and the other new horses. A little disappointed that the new Fjord was more skittish than she liked, she knew time would tell if the horse would be too nervous, or too sensitive, for their riders.

"Connor tells me," Uncle Sean reached for the butter, "even though y'all aren't open for business yet, you already have your first person signed up."

Hannah quickly swallowed the last bite from her plate. "That's right. A teen with cognitive issues. She and her mom are coming today for a look. I'd intended to set things up last night, but the fall changed my plans."

"You want a ride over?" Finn asked.

"Nah. I've got time to walk. Think through my plans."

Finn nodded. He understood the importance of quiet time before a big day.

In charge of the adaptive riding program, Hannah had way more to think through than she'd realized when she'd first signed on with her cousin for this project. She had an outstanding example to follow using the Dallas stable she'd worked at, but the amount of details involved without much support staff was almost overwhelming.

The job Connor and Catherine had done expanding the original plans to include an adaptive riding program was to be commended. Heaven knew the arena they'd built had been much bigger than anything they would have needed for a breeding stable. Still, Hannah knew they were stretching pennies to make this happen on top of building a new breeding business almost from scratch. She'd given Grace a list of possible donors she'd worked with in Dallas. It was time she reached out to a few special ones with a private note. Mrs. Marie Stewart, the grande dame of children's charities, whose granddaughter Hannah had worked with would be top on her list.

"Morning." Connor popped his head out from one of the stalls. "Didn't expect to see you here at this hour."

Hannah shrugged. "Thought I'd get an early start."

"Works for me." Connor pointed to the opposite side of the stable where the therapy horses were. A loud thumping sound carried across the cavernous structure. "Maggie is tired of waiting for her turn outside."

"So I hear." Shaking her head, Hannah crossed to the fussy horse banging the stall with her leg. "You sure are the squeaky wheel, aren't you?"

Maggie whinnied, bobbing her head up and down.

The gesture made Hannah laugh. So many people underestimated the minds and hearts of these gorgeous animals. Opening the upper half of the door, she reached in to scratch the anxious animal's chin. "Are you going to be a good girl and play nice with the others?"

Maggie kicked at the door again and stared Hannah down.

"Temper tantrums will get you nowhere fast."

The horse took a half a step back and shook her head.

"So you're going to play nice?"

This time Maggie dropped her head and let out a muffled sound before lifting her head and wiggling her lips at Hannah.

"All right." Hannah laughed out loud, opening the stall door. "You are such a charmer."

Like a good girl, Maggie followed her to the open barn door.

Stopping at the bright sunlight, Hannah gave the horse a light tap on the rump, and smiled. "Off you go."

The horse took off at a quick clip. Such elegance as her mane blew in the breeze. No matter how many times Hannah stopped to just watch, the scene was always amazing. A foot on the bottom rung of the fence, and her arms hanging over the top, she took in the animals galloping off to play at just being horses. Lord, how she loved her job.

● ● ● ●

Spooning in bed with her husband first thing in the morning was the best part of the day for Margaret 'Meg' Farraday. Well, maybe one of the best parts. And that thought brought a smile to her face. Whoever had said coffee was the best part was lying through their teeth. "Sorry, handsome, gotta get up. David is leaving today. I want to make sure he gets some of those cinnamon rolls before taking off. Maybe make him a sandwich or two."

Adam Farraday kissed his wife and slid out the other side of the bed. "Got a long day ahead of me too."

Crisscrossing in front of each other's paths, in and out of the bathroom, sharing a peck on the cheek and a quick pat on the rump rather than linger the way she'd like to, they'd hurried to dress. Meg rushed downstairs to find her guest at the front door. "Leaving already?"

"Got everything all set and ready to take off. You've been a wonderful hostess. I'll be sure to recommend this place to anybody who coming this way."

"Appreciate it, but have you had anything to eat yet?"

"No, ma'am. I'll grab something fast on the road."

Too funny, Meg thought. Poor guy had no idea. "There's no such thing as fast or on your way anywhere in this part of the country. The only place to have breakfast within a hundred miles is the café, and as good as Abbie is, it won't be that fast."

Her guest looked out the front window in the direction of the other side of town.

Watching the shift in his stance as he made up his mind and turned back to her, she wasn't willing to bet his decision was what she wanted to hear. Just in case, an extra pinch of coaxing might be in order. "Cinnamon buns are homemade. Sugar is a fast rush but at least there will be something in your stomach."

David glanced at his watch and then lifted his gaze to meet hers. His expression softened with a smile. "I guess a few more minutes won't hurt."

"Good choice." Meg spun around and hurried into the kitchen before he could change his mind.

Adam's booted heels hammered loudly as he descended the steps. "Good morning. You're still here. Good."

David turned to Adam, looking much more relaxed. "I've been bribed with fresh cinnamon rolls."

"Smart man." Sidling up behind his wife, Adam slung an arm around her waist. It had only been a few minutes since she'd been in his arms upstairs, and yet she treasured every second as if it were the first or even the last.

"Interested in some eggs to go with those rolls?" Adam asked, slowly stepping away from his wife.

David's head shifted from side to side. "I'm not really a breakfast eater. This is a treat for me."

"My sister-in-law Toni is one of the best bakers in the state of Texas, probably west of the Mississippi, and possibly across the entire country. It's going to be one hell of a treat, trust me." Adam reached for the coffee pot and holding it up, turned toward his guest. "Would you like a cup?"

"No, thanks. I want to make it straight to New Mexico without stopping."

Adam glanced down at David's hand rubbing slightly at the back of his calf. And Meg knew her husband was thinking the same thing she was. This man with an aching back last night and a sore leg this morning had no business getting on a motorcycle and riding all the way to New Mexico without stopping. He probably had no business riding to the corner.

Pushing to his feet, David removed his jacket and wiped at his forehead.

The buns in the oven and the timer set, Meg turned on her heel. David's face had paled a shade or two lighter. Even though he'd just wiped at his face, another trickle of sweat appeared between his brows.

"Guess it's going to be a scorcher today." David slung his jacket over the empty stool next to him. "Maybe a cool glass of water would be nice."

The man took two broad steps in the direction of the refrigerator, froze in place, his face pinching in pain before he smothered a loud groan and dropped hard to the ground.

"Oh my God." Meg flew around to his side, hovering close to the floor. Her husband only a half-step in front of her already had his cell phone out and on speaker.

A single tone rang out before Brooks answered, "Morning, bro."

"It's David. He began sweating profusely a few moments ago. Pale. Groaned loudly, then dropped to the floor like a two-ton anchor. He's fighting for air, so I have him sitting against the wall."

"Shit." Brooks' voice came through loud and clear. "It's that damn leg. Sounds like he's thrown a clot. Keep him upright and elevate his legs if you can. Be there in a minute."

Meg had never been so thankful to have her brother-in-law just around the corner as she was this very moment. By the time Brooks came running through the front door, medical bag in hand, Adam had removed their guest's boots and shoved two pillows under his legs.

Brooks bent down and lifted first the right leg and then the left, shoving his hand under the jeans up to the knee. "Just what I expected. That area behind his left knee is warm, and he flinched when I touched it. Classic phlebitis symptom. Probably brought on by the long motorcycle ride with his knees bent the entire time."

Standing out of the way, Meg hugged herself watching her

brother-in-law pull a vial from his medicine bag and quickly fill a hypodermic needle.

Brooks grabbed an IV from his medical kit and pushed the entire syringe full of medicine into it. "Go find me something to hang this on. The faster we get the Heparin into him the better." No sooner had the words left his mouth than he was placing a tourniquet on David's arm and searching for a vein.

Just as Meg returned with a hat rack from the hallway, he had an IV needle in place and quickly adjusted the flow of the life-saving medicine to wide open. "Let's get him off the floor. The sofa will have to do for now. Be careful not to jar the needle." Brooks slid an arm underneath his patient's shoulders, Adam came from the other side, and Meg hurried forward just in case she could help make a difference. Together the three of them maneuvered the man into the other room and set him down on the couch as comfortably as possible for a man of his height. "Damn good thing you didn't let him out the door. Had he thrown a clot on route out of town there's no way in hell he'd be breathing now."

"Have to go." David's voice came out low and rough, his eyes remained closed.

Meg squatted beside him. "Don't worry. No hurries. You need to take care of yourself."

"Can't stay." Eyes still shut, David waved the arm with the IV in the air and thrust the other in the opposite direction, knocking Meg off her feet.

"David," Brooks shouted, sounding more like a drill sergeant than a doctor.

"Go," David muttered and nearly twisted off the sofa. Adam and Meg scrambled to keep the man from hurting himself.

"Shit." Brooks reached into the bag beside him and grabbed the pre-filled syringe that he kept handy for just this kind of situation. Quickly, he injected the Versed into the IV tubing, and within seconds, David's shoulders relaxed and his eyes closed.

"Is he going to be okay?" Meg tried desperately to keep her tone calmer than she felt.

"I hope to hell so." Brooks placed three fingers on the sleeping man's wrist and nodded.

Meg didn't have a clue who this man was, if he had family, or people who cared about him, but right now she was frantic enough with worry for all of them.

CHAPTER SIX

"How did I let you talk me into this?" Hannah pulled into an empty space at the café.

"You've worked non-stop day and night. After that fall you took yesterday—"

"I'm fine."

"Yes, but you still deserve a break. You put in a couple of hours with the horses this morning and now it's time for a little R&R."

Knowing better than to argue with her aunt was probably why Hannah was here in the first place. And maybe, just maybe, a small hope at a second chance to bump into last night's stranger. Perhaps if she had another opportunity to visit, to talk, she could get some closure and put this guy out of her head once and for all. On the other hand, she wasn't a daydreaming teen anymore, what she should do is stop letting her imagination run away with her and move on with real life.

"It's about time you got here." Sally May waved for her friend to hurry up. "Ruth Ann is just about to deal."

"Deal Hannah in, too." Without skipping a beat, Aunt Eileen was in her seat and scooping up the cards.

"Any word on how Grace's trip to Houston is going?" Ruth Ann asked as she dealt.

"Nothing much. You know how Houston is—"

"Humid," Dorothy and Sally May cut her off and the entire table laughed.

"Sure hope she gets a chance to check up on the Thompsons between rubbing elbows with the rest of those hotshot lawyers and horsemen."

Aunt Eileen fanned her cards. "Oh, I'm sure she will."

Nora, Brooks' nurse, smiled up at Hannah. "I see you got roped into a game."

"Wasn't that hard." Hannah smiled back.

"I bet," Nora said through a chuckle at the same moment her phone sounded with a text. "Hm."

Before Nora could fish her cell out of her purse, Aunt Eileen's cell dinged as well. Not much reason for concern in a city where folks were glued to their phones with the same fascination as a passerby and a car wreck, but in Tuckers Bluff, where folks still preferred to drop in for a visit than to call, the synchronized timing was curious.

"Damn." Nora jumped to her feet. "Best hand I've had all morning." She dropped her cards on the table. "We've got an emergency. I need to go."

Aunt Eileen's brows buckled with concern. "DJ wants us at the B&B."

"That's where the emergency is." Nora slung her purse over her shoulder. "Guess I'll see you there."

Aunt Eileen nodded, and looked at Hannah. "We'd better haul ass."

"We'll hold the table down till you get back," Ruth Ann called. It wouldn't be the first time three of the social club ladies kept a game going.

Hurrying to the car, Hannah hit the unlock fob. "What's going on?"

"DJ didn't say."

"Only one way to find out." Hannah turned the ignition, backed out of the space, and as her aunt had said a few minutes ago, hauled ass down the street.

At the B&B, Hannah took the porch steps two at a time. The only thing stopping her heart from pounding out of its chest was knowing if any of the family were in trouble, Aunt Eileen would have gotten a phone call not a text. At least that's what Hannah kept telling herself.

The first thing to grab her attention was Nora in the front

parlor hovering over a lump on the sofa. What had her and her aunt moving on to the big living room was the sound of her cousins' voices increasing in decibel.

"What the hell is going on?" Aunt Eileen came to a stop in the middle of the room.

"We have a situation," DJ said.

Brooks glared at his brother. "Not if we don't make it one."

"Butler Springs is not an option," DJ countered.

Brooks whipped his stethoscope from around his neck and tossed it on the sofa. "And the ranch is?"

"With limited information, this is the most logical step."

"No." Brooks shook his head vehemently.

"Maybe," Aunt Eileen stepped between her two nephews, "y'all should let me in on why you're bickering like a couple of young bucks."

The two brothers stared at each other for a moment longer than Hannah was comfortable with. She'd seen the wrath of Aunt Eileen growing up and didn't put it past the woman to haul both grown men off to the woodshed.

Brooks was the first to ease his stance, rubbing the back of his neck as he spoke to his aunt. "Your dinner guest from last night threw a clot this morning."

"Oh, my." Aunt Eileen's hand flew to her mouth.

"He needs to be monitored. Have daily blood tests," he turned to his brother, "in a hospital," then faced his aunt again. "It will be at least a few days before the prescription blood thinners kick in. Until then we need to keep him on a Heparin IV."

"He's not in a hospital now and he's stable." DJ spun around and faced his aunt. "Here's the deal. I spoke last night with David—who by the way, usually goes by Dale. He's supposed to be under the radar."

Aunt Eileen's lips tightened into a thin line.

DJ continued, "I'm concerned if he checks into a hospital, any hospital—"

"He won't be under the radar anymore," Aunt Eileen finished.

"Exactly. It's also probably best if the whole town doesn't know he's still here."

This exact scenario could have been taking place in Hannah's family house. Only in her case the one asking for special favors would be Jamie, the free spirit, and the one arguing for following the rules would be Ian, the by-the-book lawman. And of course, the one making the final decision, probably in Jamie's favor, would be her mom.

Aunt Eileen spun around to face her other nephew. "Can we keep an eye on him at the ranch?"

Eyes closed, Brooks blew out a sigh before leveling his gaze with his aunt. "It could be done. We can do Heparin shots, but it's not optimal."

Spinning about to face DJ again, Aunt Eileen seemed to weigh what both men had shared. "Will this be putting anyone in harm's way?"

DJ paused longer than Hannah was comfortable with. Of all the crazy things she'd come up with in her lifetime, and a few had been whoppers, none would have put anyone in any kind of danger.

"It's a possibility, but I think it's low. If I learn different..." He let his words hang.

"I'll have to talk to your father, but in this family we do because we can. As long as we know what we're up against we can certainly take care of ourselves. If it comes down to it, we all know how to use a gun."

DJ sighed and nodded. Hannah knew Aunt Eileen and guns were a sore spot in the family.

"I don't see any reason Sean will say anything different," Aunt Eileen continued. "I have a good feeling about that young man. If it's all right with your father, it's all right with me." And if her Uncle Sean was anything like Hannah's dad and her mom, whatever was right with Aunt Eileen would be fine with Uncle Sean.

● ● ● ●

Dale had the mother of all headaches.

"Don't move," a soft voice urged.

Maybe if he was really lucky, the voice was that of an angel and this mess of a life as he knew it was over. Taking way more energy than it should have, he managed to open his eyes. Or at least one of them.

"Hi," the angelic voice said. This time there was a face to go with the words. A pretty face. A familiar face. "You've had a rough day."

Had he? Struggling to focus more clearly, he let his gaze skip over the pretty face and glance around. Nothing else seemed even remotely familiar. The pleasant homey room implied he wasn't in any danger. Steely blue eyes narrowed at his prolonged silence and it dawned on him he should say something. "Hi." Not exactly Shakespeare, but what did they say about less is more.

"Stay still, I'm going to get my cousin." Quick-paced steps disappeared down what sounded like wooden stairs.

Cousin? This time his gaze turned to the IV in his arm and then scanned the room again. The place didn't look a thing like any hospital he'd ever been in. Why couldn't he remember where he was, or how he got here? The last thing he recalled was talking with DJ. No. Breakfast and the fabulous smell of fresh baking cinnamon rolls. Then nothing. He was still wracking his memory for more details when multiple footsteps pounded in his direction.

The door eased open and the angel, no not an angel, DJ's cousin came in the door with a DJ clone. "You look better than you should."

"Thanks." Though that wasn't the first word that had come to mind.

"I'm Brooks Farraday. Remember me from last night?"

Barely, but Dale nodded anyhow.

The good doctor pushed the bottom end of the bed sheet to one side and reached under Dale's left leg, nodding. "Good. Not so warm anymore. You threw a clot."

A flash of recollected pain came to him. "My leg."

Brooks nodded. "I noted signs of recent injuries."

Not a question. Dale didn't bother nodding.

"Your doctor should have warned you that several hours on a motorcycle with your legs locked in a single position is just asking for a problem."

This time Dale nodded. The doctor had mentioned several similar things when they'd made the switch.

"Now you're grounded."

"Grounded?" What the hell was the guy talking about?

"You've been on an IV of Heparin to prevent more clots. You're damn lucky we got this under control quickly. Had I not noticed you rubbing your leg last night, had my brother not noticed you sweating and called me right away, had I not placed the Heparin in my bag, you would probably be dead now."

Dale wasn't a doctor but even he knew what a blood clot to the heart or lung could do and how fast it could kill a person. "Thanks."

"That's my job." The hint of a smile took the edge off his words. Another humble Farraday. And another one that Dale was very pleased he was better than good at his job.

"Now what?" He needed to get moving. Out of town. Out of Texas.

"My brother seems convinced putting you in the hospital isn't in your best interest. I'm going to remove the IV. You have a prescription for blood thinners to take until your next check up with your regular physician. We'll do injections for a few days until there's enough of the Warfarin, the prescription, in your system for you to ride off into the sunset again."

"No." Setting the un-needled arm at his side to shove off the bed with, Dale paused at the soft grip on his shoulder.

"Not a good idea," the angel whispered.

"She's right. Like it or not, it will take time for the blood thinner pills to kick in. Even after that, you'll still need to be under a doctor's care to stabilize the meds and blood clots. Then—"

"Stop. That sounds like a lot more time than I have."

"You like breathing?" Brooks asked.

Dale remained quiet.

"Then you take the time."

"I can't check into a hospital."

"You're not." The angel smiled at him. "You'll be staying here. Brooks is going to monitor you."

"Where exactly is here?"

"You're at the ranch house. I'm sure you'll be way more comfortable here than at the hospital in Butler Springs."

"I can't do this either." He knew she was right. He'd be a lot more comfortable here. And he knew the doctor was right, getting on his motorcycle was not the best idea. But he knew even more importantly, staying here was most definitely not a good plan.

"It's DJ's idea."

"DJ?" Had his friend lost his mind?

Brooks nodded. "That was my first thought too. But whatever you and my brother are not telling me, starting with why you gave us a different name, he seems to think this is the best place for you."

Maybe a few years in the country had made DJ soft. That had to be the only answer. Once again trying to push off his free arm, Dale raised himself upright. The stiffness in his back and pin prickle sensation in his leg reinforced the notion that staying put was in his best interest. But since when did he do what was in his best interest? "Thank you, Miss—"

"Hannah."

That's right. "Thank you, Hannah." He went to sling his legs over the side of the bed and realized his pants were nowhere in sight.

"If you're looking for your britches," Aunt Eileen came into the room carrying a tray, "forget about it. They had to cut them off you."

"I have more in my bag." Less concerned with where he was,

he took another look around the room for his bag.

"I'm sure you do." Aunt Eileen set the tray on a nearby dresser and turned to face him. "Now you get back into the bed and raise your legs. You do exactly as you're told because you are in my charge now, young man, and nothing is going to happen to you on my watch."

Dale came within seconds of arguing with the older woman when muffled laughter reached him. Taking unexpected interest in the ceiling, Hannah stood to one side, her fingers over her mouth in an effort to better hide her amusement. Brooks, on the other hand, wore a satisfied smirk. Something told Dale that arguing would get him nowhere. The question at hand now was how did he explain to these nice but misguided people that it was in their best interest to give him his pants and let him go?

CHAPTER SEVEN

Now things were starting to get interesting. Hannah kept to herself as Aunt Eileen set the drink and dish on the night table.

Clearly ready to leave, Brooks snapped his bag shut and looked at Dale. "Hannah and Aunt Eileen have instructions on what you can and can't do. I'll be by tomorrow to check up on you. DJ will be by tonight. Until then I suggest you just go with the flow." Shaking his head, Brooks didn't wait for a response. He turned, gave his aunt a kiss on the cheek, then Hannah, and headed straight for the door. "Remember, if Aunt Eileen isn't happy, nobody is happy."

Sitting upright with the sheet wrapped around his waist, Dale painted a very pretty picture. Well, maybe not pretty. Perhaps handsome was a better word. Or maybe hunky. Or maybe calendar material. Or maybe Hannah should stop thinking about how good-looking this guy sitting in front of her was and start thinking about how he almost died this morning. Then she could start to wonder about why he was so anxious to get the hell away from Tuckers Bluff and why DJ was so anxious to keep him here and the town thinking he'd left. Whatever the case was, her aunt could handle it for now. "I'll let you two decide who's going to win this round. I want to pop over a minute to Connor's and check on Starburst again."

"You go ahead, sweetie." Aunt Eileen held a glass of water out to their guest. "We'll be just fine." She leveled her gaze with Dale. "Won't we?"

Mr. Hunky barely blinked. Nodding, he lifted his leg back onto the bed and let Aunt Eileen help him adjust the pillows before accepting the water. Whatever happened over the next few days,

Hannah decided this could prove to be the most entertainment she'd had in a long time.

Her foot hit the bottom step just as Brooks opened the front door. "You want to give me a lift over to Connor's?"

The way he glanced up the stairs and back, Hannah thought for a moment he was going to say no. "Sure, no problem."

"You're really worried about him, aren't you?" She wasn't referring to just the man's medical condition and Brooks knew it.

"I'm not sure yet." Brooks held the door open for her and stepped aside. "There's just enough I don't understand to make me want to know a whole lot more before letting this guy spend even another hour in this house. On the other hand, I trust my brother with my life, and if DJ says this is the best thing for everybody, I won't argue with him." He shifted his bag from one hand to the other and gestured for her to lead the way. "Might as well get moving."

Up until a few seconds ago Hannah was anxious to get back to the stables since Connor had brought in more horses than she had expected for potential therapy rides. Once Grace had started seriously working on the nonprofit end of the adaptive riding business, the entire family had been overwhelmed by the amount of interest and need in this part of the state. Everyone had assumed this far out in the middle of nowhere they'd be limited by whom they could help. As it turns out, plenty of people were willing to drive insane distances to get good help for their loved ones.

As excited as she was with every inquiry, new horse, new piece of equipment, new board nailed into place and every inch of the program coming together, and as much as she wanted to go and work the stable now, suddenly the thought of leaving Aunt Eileen alone in the house didn't sit right with her. "On second thought, the horses will still be there in the morning." As her cousin had done a few seconds before, she looked up the stairway and back. "Besides, Aunt Eileen may need some help."

Brooks smiled at his young cousin. "Aren't we the pair of worrywarts?"

A puff of dust kicked up in the distance. A parade of cars turned onto the long driveway. Shading her eyes with her hand, Hannah squinted to get a better look. The sight almost made her laugh. "Looks like we're not the only two. That's Sally Mae's car leading the pack. My guess is the rest of the social club is following in tow."

"You and I may be worried. The rest of those ladies are overprotective on steroids. But I do feel better having a houseful of people here."

Hannah nodded in agreement. "You're probably right."

"Still want a ride?" Brooks offered again.

"Nah," Hannah took a step back, hiding from view, "I think I'll stick around. Things might get a bit interesting."

"Suit yourself. But just in case, if any of them come bearing cake balls...." He glanced over to the first car pulling up in front of the house and shook his head, holding back a smile. "Lock the guns and run for the hills."

"Got it, cuz." Hannah really did love being around so much family again. Jamie and Ian had left home so long ago that she often felt like an only child. All this concern mingled with humor reminded her of her own family when she was a kid. "If things get really rough I'll send up smoke signals."

Still shaking his head, Brooks made a mad dash for his car, pausing a moment to wave at the ladies as they one by one slammed their car doors and made their way to the house.

Hannah closed the door and hurried up the stairs. Whatever the plan was to keep the presence of the new house guest under wraps, she was pretty sure none of it included an afternoon call from the Tuckers Bluff Ladies Afternoon Social Club.

• • • •

"Y'all didn't have to come all the way out here." Eileen repositioned her playing cards.

Ruth Ann looked to her friend. "The way you and Hannah

took off this morning—"

"That was nothing." Eileen tightened her grip on her cards. If they were going to pull this off, distracting these women for the next couple of hours would be key. "Poor Meg was just all aflutter over her guest passing out."

Sally Mae threw a chip into the pot. "I'd have thought Meg was made of stronger stuff than that. On the other hand, it can be rather frightening to have a supposedly healthy person suddenly drop at your feet. Good thing for everyone it was just his blood sugar."

Eileen focused on her cards. The last thing she needed was for her friends to see on her face the fib that the young man had recovered and ridden out of town.

"But what really got me worrying," Sally Mae continued, "was Hannah feeling poorly enough that the two of you skipped our game and headed home. Especially with her just having taken that fall yesterday."

"It was a new horse so she didn't know his quirks yet. Dragging her into town too soon was my fault. I should've made her take it easy today." Eileen rearranged her cards for the umpteenth time. "But I've taken care of that now. Hannah is installed nice and cozy upstairs with a barrage of pillows, lots of snacks and plenty of DVDs." An ace peeked out from behind a playing card. She needed to grab her thoughts and pay more attention to her hand, only right now her mind was more concerned with the pretense of a sickly Hannah and wondering what the heck was going on upstairs. "After this hand I'll check on her."

"Better take more food." Sally May laughed. "Bump on the head or not that girl is always hungry."

Eileen chuckled in earnest. The girl did eat like one of the boys.

Since Brooks' nurse Nora lived in town, she hadn't come to the ranch with Brooks or the other ladies, which was probably a good thing. It was bad enough Eileen was pretty much lying through her teeth to her best friends, no point in putting poor Nora on the spot too. It was best for everyone to forget about the stranger and believe him long gone. But as soon as her nephew got home tonight, Eileen was going to get at the root of what in the name of heavens all this secrecy was about. Tight-lipped was one thing, but this complicated mess was bordering on ridiculous.

• • • •

This jam was going from bad to worse. Dale should have boarded a plane to Brazil and called it a day. All he had meant to do was drive through Tuckers Bluff, pop into the police station for five minutes, and let DJ, the only other person he'd trust with his life, know that he was indeed alive and well. Then he was supposed to get on his bike and ride into the sunset. Untraceable. No one to be the wiser. Instead, he'd landed smack dab in the center of the Farraday home.

Despite the limited information he'd shared last night, he'd been positive DJ understood the gravity of the situation. What Dale didn't understand was, if DJ got that Dale was in trouble enough to keep him in hiding, why in heaven's name would DJ insist he do it at the family home?

Hannah cleared her throat. "Are you going to play, or just stare at your hand until the next millennium?"

"Sorry. Do you have any twos?"

"Go fish." Hannah grinned over the rim of her cards.

Maybe he was the one who had lost his mind. After all he was in a room alone with an attractive woman—on his bed no less—and he was playing a kid's card game. Not even the strip version. He hadn't played Go Fish the right way since kindergarten. But so far, she'd creamed him at poker, annihilated him at Rummy, conquered him at War, and now the only unskilled game he stood a chance at winning had dwindled down to Go Fish.

"Do you have any threes?" Hannah asked.

"You know I do." He handed over his cards. The woman should play Vegas. Even dumb luck wasn't in his favor. "You don't have to babysit me. I promise I won't run away from home."

"It's not that." She shifted her cards frowning. "Have any tens?"

"Go fish. Then what is it?"

"I told you. Aunt Eileen plays poker Saturday mornings in town. Since she skipped the card game they brought the card game to her."

"Yes, I got that, if Mohammed won't go to the mountain, the mountain will go to Mohammed. And I understand that no one outside of the family is to know that I am staying here." That was just about the only thing he'd been told since he woke up that made any sense to him. On top of his other concerns, he doubted DJ's logic in telling the family his real name was Dale, and he had no clue how this would play out when Grace returned from her trip. No one else in the family knew him, but Grace was another story. "And you've been designated the guard keeper."

"Not really. The only excuse my aunt could come up with quickly for the two of us not staying in town was that I wasn't feeling well after yesterday's fall. So by having me stay up here, she has an excuse to come check on you without making any of the ladies wonder why she keeps coming up and down the stairs."

"I understand, but she doesn't have to come up to check on me, so you could have stayed downstairs and played cards. I'll be fine."

The pretty woman in front of him laughed a tad too loud and slapped her hand over her mouth before speaking through her fingers. "For sure you don't know Aunt Eileen. Like it or not, until you get a clean bill of health and traveling orders, you will be under her eagle eye. So, for now, we're stuck here until the ladies go home." She closed her cards and set them down. "How's the leg feeling?"

"Not bad." Considering the dumb thing had almost killed him, it felt pretty good. He really was anxious to get moving, yet at the same time he liked the idea of sticking around. Liked the idea of being with people who cared. Liked the idea of playing cards with

Hannah. And he knew better than to be thinking of her as anything other than an off-limits member of DJ's family. Watching the way she treated her horse yesterday, he could tell she had a good heart. And her willingly, and cheerfully, staying locked up with him in this room without complaint only confirmed that assumption. She was a nice kid. Well, maybe kid wasn't quite accurate. But still, any other place, any other time, and he'd enjoy really getting to know her. Another good reason why moving on as soon as possible was the best idea he'd had in the last few days.

"They're gone." Aunt Eileen came through the door. "And boy am I glad. Couldn't keep that one up any longer. Lost the last three pots on purpose, which," she put one hand on her hip and waved a finger at Hannah, "is not easy to do when you get a royal flush."

"Ooh," Dale whistled. "Man, that must have hurt."

Aunt Eileen grinned. "It did. And I feel better knowing you appreciate the sacrifice I made."

"Why did you throw the game?" Hannah asked.

Shaking her head, Aunt Eileen scooped up the empty glass from the bedside table. "Hated pretending. Finally said I was too distracted with you up here to enjoy the game." She shrugged. "At least that was mostly the truth. Didn't mention I was distracted by two of you."

Hannah's aunt wasn't the only one. Which was probably why he'd done his best to keep the conversation during his confinement strictly about card games.

"I think," Aunt Eileen eyed Dale from head to toe, "we can let you downstairs to rest on the sofa as easily as up here."

Pushing himself upright, Dale had to hold back a grin at the two women hovering on either side of him as though he were at risk to self-combust. No wonder Declan Farraday was so well adjusted. Who the hell wouldn't be having grown up with Mary Poppins and Florence Nightingale?

CHAPTER EIGHT

Hannah stood in the living room with two cups of tea waiting for Aunt Eileen to stuff another pillow under Dale's legs. If she lifted them up any higher the man was going to be standing on his head. "I think that's enough, Aunt Eileen." The man didn't say anything, but the twinkle in his eye and the grin tugging at the corners of his mouth told her that he thought the same thing.

Taking a step back and letting her hands fall to her waist, Aunt Eileen surveyed her houseguest, squinted slightly, then shaking her head leaned over and pulled the pillow out from underneath him. "Three pillows is enough." Without another word, she turned and walked to the kitchen.

Both Hannah and Dale kept their eyes on her aunt's exiting back until she turned out of sight.

"She's thorough, I'll give her that." Looking over his shoulder to make sure Aunt Eileen couldn't see him, Dale pulled the top cushion out from under his leg.

"She means well. But my mom is the same way. Sometimes they just don't know when to stop. They seem to have gotten an extra mother-hen gene."

"There are a lot of people who probably wish they had a mother in their life with that extra gene."

"Don't get me wrong. I love my Aunt Eileen almost as much as I love my own mother. Growing up I spent more time in the summer here than I did at home. In this family, a Farraday is a Farraday. And I can't imagine having grown up anywhere else with anyone else. Not a lot of people would give up living in the big city, or at least as big as Dallas is, to work with cousins and aunts and uncles out in the middle of what most people consider nowhere."

"But you're not a lot of people, are you?" The corners of Dale's lips lifted into a full-blown smile.

"Nope." She took a sip of her tea. "Those same people who wouldn't give up their lives in the city have no clue what they're missing."

Dale cocked his head to one side. "What are they missing?"

Hannah had to think about that a minute. She knew what the answer was for herself—family, community, and horses. While everybody needed family and community, she'd be crazy to think everybody needed horses. "Our lives have become fast-paced, hectic, and intense. Our minds are on constant overload with cell phones and computer screens and electronic gadgets. Out here, people work hard so they can enjoy their life. In the city people work hard so they can pay the bills."

"Not everybody," Dale said. "I know a lot of people who love the work they do. Working long and hard is enjoying life for them."

"Agreed. I'm one of the lucky ones who works at something I absolutely loved. The people who worked with me got to do what they loved. But too many of them had to work second jobs at things they didn't love that ate up their hours to afford things that used to come more easily with a simple lifestyle."

"That sounds a bit cynical."

Hannah shrugged. "Maybe it's just a case of you can take the girl out of the country, but you can't take the country out of the girl."

Nodding, Dale studied her so long that she almost shifted in place to break the connection. Playing cards upstairs, the moments of occasional silence seemed normal, comfortable, pleasant. For some reason, being downstairs in the open living room, the silence felt awkward. Which of course made absolutely no sense at all. Where she should have felt awkward was alone with a near stranger on a bed behind closed doors. Maybe she was just losing her mind. Or had drunk too much sweet tea. After all everyone knew sugar was not the best thing for you. Maybe.

Hannah stood. Her aunt was perfectly capable of catering to a pleasant houseguest. And she wanted to check out another horse. "If you'll excuse me. I'd like to do a quick run over to Connor's."

Dale swung his legs over the side of the sofa. "Great. I'll come with you."

"I don't think that's a good idea. Our instructions were for you to take it easy today."

"Take it easy, yes. Vegetate, no." Dale stood up. "It's a blood clot. I'm on blood thinners, movement is good for me."

"I'm not so sure about that one."

"I am. Trust me." He glanced down at his laced footwear. "I don't know where my boots are. Is this good enough?"

"Just don't stand near the horses." Now all she had to figure out was how to convince her aunt to let this man loose. Or maybe she should just get him back on the sofa and sit on him if necessary to keep him still. Suddenly a vivid picture of her straddling a six foot handsome hunk flashed in front of her, making walking in running shoes near thousand pound horses sound like a really safe idea. She was most definitely going to have to accept Andy's invitation to dinner the next time he asked. So what if he's a funeral director?

• • • •

"Oh boy, am I glad you're here." Connor Farraday came strutting out of the barn to greet Hannah and Dale. "Looks like you're doing better."

"I see word gets around fast here," Dale said.

Connor shrugged. "Need to know basis."

Dale avoided the instinct to shift like a trapped animal. The scrutiny in Connor's eyes was clear. Dale wasn't sure how much DJ had told his family, but from the way Connor looked at him, it was enough to garner their cooperation to accept him into the fold, but not enough to satisfy all their burning questions. He couldn't blame Connor or any of the others. He had a few burning questions for DJ of his own.

Connor faced his cousin. "I got a call from Adele Hampton."

"Hampton?"

"That's the lady who lives in Midland. The only equine therapist her son liked working with moved to California. According to her, since the therapist left, he's been surly and difficult and unable to get along with any other therapist in Midland, or pretty much anyone else. She feels they're back to square one. Sounds pretty frustrated. "

"I bet." Hannah snapped her fingers. "Now I remember. Mrs. Stewart referred her to me."

"Yes. And apparently, they decided today would be a good day to drive out here and meet you."

"You've got to be kidding?" Hannah's jaw almost hit the floor. "That's pretty darn short notice."

"It's worse than that." Connor gestured apologetically with his hands. "She's about thirty minutes out."

"Thirty minutes? What if I were out of town today? Or had the flu? What was she planning on doing then?"

"I get the impression that this woman is used to getting what she wants."

Hannah glanced from Connor to the barn's open arena door, then over to Dale and back to her cousin. "I suppose if she just wants to talk it's not a big deal. But if she wants to see me in action, I don't have any therapy students."

"I tried to tell her that. But she was very insistent. Polite. But insistent. And I'm sorry kid, but I promised Ken Brady I'd be there half an hour ago to help with their new horse. I can't put it off any longer."

"No, no. You go on. I can handle this woman." Hannah spun around on her boot heel and smiled up at Dale. "You got any experience with horses?"

"Only the kind under a hood."

"That'll have to do. You're about to get a crash course on the kind with four legs."

Her words barely had time to process, when Dale found himself rushing to catch up to her.

"Thankfully everything in the arena is ready to go. Structurally that is. But I don't have any training elements out. If you'll help me, we'll set up the stage."

"I'm all yours."

"Good." Grinning, she glanced over her shoulder at him. "But for both our sakes, you better not say a word to Aunt Eileen."

That much he didn't have a problem with. What he was finding a little challenging was the cute way one side of her mouth tipped slightly higher than the other when she tried to hide a full-fledged grin. Though it was safer watching her smile than looking at the rest of her.

On the other side of the arena he followed her to a large storage room. Hannah moved with deliberate intent. Her focus was intense. It was surprisingly fascinating to watch her reach, grab, and carry what to him looked like swimming pool noodles, and when her arms were full she'd pass them off to him.

"Take these to the arena for me, set them down inside the door, then come back. We'll load up with as many of the props as we can. It shouldn't take too long to set up the training course. Hopefully we'll have at least enough to give a good impression to Mrs. Hampton of how things will be and what we can do."

Dale didn't say a word. He simply nodded, accepted the noodles that were considerably heavier than he had expected, and spun back in the direction she'd told him.

He wasn't exactly sure how much time passed as the two spread the noodles of different sizes and patterns at different sections of the arena. All patterns were set up around two main squares, one on either side of the arena.

"And how does this help the person on the horse?" He didn't mean to seem dense, but he wasn't following why leading a horse in and out of a square on the ground could somehow help a person with physical or emotional issues.

"That depends on the person. See those letters scattered on the wall?" She waited for him to nod. "The rider will stop at each and count to three then walk on to the next. All of these things are designed to help cognitive students with sequencing."

"What about someone with a physical injury?"

"There are a lot of different reasons why therapeutic riding can help. For instance, a horse's hips move the same way ours do. This creates involuntary muscle memory and strength without the rider's knowledge, so they can improve and grow strong doing something fun."

"So say you have a stubborn teen who doesn't want to do his regular therapy, riding a horse can make a difference. I think I get it."

"Good, because we've got about ten minutes left and it can take more than that to saddle up Maggie."

"Maggie?"

"She's a good horse. She's not terribly fond of men so you'll have to keep your distance, but she's great with children."

"Your eyes light up when you talk about Maggie."

"I love that animal more than some people love their own family."

That didn't seem so hard to believe. He knew as well as the next cop that too many people didn't have a clue what family meant, never mind love and respect.

Inside the barn area, Hannah stopped in a room similar to the storage room she'd gotten the props from. This room contained saddles, harnesses, all sorts of blankets, and leather horse things hung from the walls and on the shelves. With the same military precision she had used walking through the other area, she reached for what she wanted and handed things off to Dale. Even loaded with gear, including a bucket with brushes looped on his fingers, he instinctively lurched forward when she grabbed for what he knew had to be a heavy saddle.

"Don't go macho on me. I've been carrying saddles since I was old enough to sit in one. Follow me." Without hesitation, she turned and marched out the door and down the hall. Halfway down the stalls she eased her step. "You'd better wait here." She set the saddle over what looked like a carpenter's sawhorse and took the bucket and a few other things from his arms. "I'm going to clean her up quickly and then come get the saddle."

"Are you sure I can't help?"

"Yeah, I won't be long."

Despite that she couldn't see him with her back to him, he nodded, even though the last thing he wanted was to wait on the sidelines. Not that he had a problem taking orders from a woman. He'd done that in the Marines and he did that on the police force. Heck, he'd been taking orders from his mother most of his life. But something about the way this young woman took command, especially in what many people would consider a man's world, made him want to follow her anywhere. Even to hell and back.

CHAPTER NINE

"**D**on't we have our hands full?" Hannah pulled a treat from her pocket and held her palm out to Maggie. Back home she'd rescued the horse from a less caring owner. But it had been the jackass before that who had left Maggie gun shy of most men. "You like those, don't you?"

Maggie gave a nod of her head before nudging up beside Hannah. Even though she was in a hurry, she took an extra second to scratch under the mare's chin. Making quick work of brushing off any dust and picking out the horse's hooves, Hannah moved to her neck, reaching for the mane and tail comb in her pocket and realized she must have left it with Dale. Giving Maggie a small rub behind her ear, Hannah whispered, "Be right back, girl."

She came to a stop in front of Dale and his empty hands. Blast. "I must have left the comb in the tack room. Wait here, I'll be right back."

Dale gave her a nod, but like a few moments ago, said nothing. She picked up her pace, nearly trotting to the tack room, her mind bouncing around with multiple ideas. She needed to hurry. She didn't like to leave Maggie alone in her stall half ready to ride, and she needed to make a good impression on Mrs. Hampton so the woman would give a good report to Mrs. Stewart before Hannah reached out to her for a donation. But more than anything, the thing bouncing back and forth in her thoughts was how much she wished Dale had actually spoken his response. Something in the timbre of his voice struck a nerve. A good nerve. She hadn't realized how much she enjoyed hearing it, until he stopped speaking. And wasn't that the silliest thing you ever heard. She was a full-blown grown-up now, had been for years, and yet she was thinking and behaving like a besotted teen. She seriously needed to get out and socialize more.

Grabbing the comb she'd dropped, she spun and hurried out the door toward the stall. For a quick second she wondered where Dale had gone. Even took another second to glance behind her to see if he'd wandered off to visit a different horse. Not till she was almost to Maggie's stall did she hear the voice she had missed.

Her heart rate galloped as quickly as Maggie could cross an open field. And yet, it wasn't adding up. A man in Maggie's stall would have the horse kicking up her feet, knocking into the sides and making a whole heck of a lot of noise. The poor horse had almost been put down after badly hurting a stable hand who had ignored the sign on the door warning men to keep out.

Scared of what she might find, and completely confused over the soft voice and the quiet horse, Hannah approached the stall with caution. For a second she even considered that perhaps Maggie had gotten out and made her way to the pasture and Dale was simply standing there talking to himself. Not the case. Almost afraid to breathe, she peaked around to see Dale at the horse's side, scratching her chin and whispering so softly Hannah could barely make out his next words. The timbre of his voice, the fluctuations in his tone, a gentleness that could have put a sacrificial lamb at ease, all worked together to instantly soothe any concerns she might have had. Obviously Dale's voice was having the same effect on Maggie.

If not for the sound of clacking heels in the distance, Hannah would've gladly stood outside the stall for the rest of the day listening to that low murmur. Lowering her voice and moving forward slowly, she approached. "It sounds like Mrs. Hampton is here. I need to go greet her. Why don't you come with me?"

Dale switched from scratching to gently stroking the horse's neck. "Of course."

Waiting for him to exit before her, Hannah couldn't decide where to start. Whether to raise the roof over his having disobeyed her instructions, or to bow at his feet in awe of how he managed to get inside the stall without upsetting Maggie. She didn't have time for either as she could see Mrs. Hampton walking toward them at a quick clip with Catherine at her side.

"There you are," Catherine said with her public relations smile firmly in place.

"We were getting one of the horses ready to ride," Hannah said.

Mrs. Hampton glanced up and over. "Very nice. But that won't be necessary today."

"We're very proud of what we've built here." Catherine continued to smile.

"Connor has spared no expense to create the best possible adaptive riding stable," Hannah added.

"Yes, that's what Mrs. Farraday here," Mrs. Hampton gestured to her left, "has been explaining to us. Mrs. Stewart spoke very highly of you. But my son's problems are very different from her granddaughter's."

"Therapy or adaptive riding works wonders for a wide variation of people in multiple situations." Hannah joined her cousin in flashing the perfect smile.

"Yes, well broken bones will heal in time. But not so with the rest of the human psyche."

It took an extra bit of effort for Hannah not to flinch at Mrs. Hampton's words. Mrs. Stewart's granddaughter had more than a few broken bones. She'd been badly injured in a car accident and had been challenged to improve muscle strength coordination and mental acuity. The will to move had been there but her mind and her body had somehow misconnected. Her bones had healed long ago.

"I have some work to do in my office." Catherine took a step back. "If you will excuse me, Mrs. Hampton, Hannah can show you whatever you would like to see."

The woman in casual attire that Hannah knew had probably cost as much as her monthly salary, smiled politely at Catherine and turned to face Dale. "And you are?"

"I'm here to help."

"Oh, a volunteer." This time she gave the man more of her attention, sizing him up so casually that most people might not have noticed what she'd done. Whatever she had seen she must have liked because the plastic society smile she'd worn since coming into the stables bloomed with sincerity.

"Yes, ma'am." Dale returned the smile.

"Shall we take a look at the arena?" Hannah asked.

Mrs. Hampton nodded. "Yes, that is why I came."

Leading the way, Hannah walked between Mrs. Hampton and Dale. "I thought you might be bringing your son."

"I did."

"Oh." Hannah blinked quickly, looking around the open spaces.

"He wouldn't get out of the car." The woman's voice was harsher but Hannah recognized it as mostly frustration. "I'll try again after I've looked around. Or better yet," she stopped to face Dale, "why don't you go see if you can talk my son into joining us? He's probably tired of women telling him what to do."

"I…" Dale cast a furtive glance in Hannah's direction, a silent plea for what to do.

She didn't like it but there wasn't much she could say or do now besides offer a silent hint of a nod. They needed a good report to get back to Mrs. Stewart.

"Very well," Dale continued, "I can certainly try. Where did you park?"

Mrs. Hampton pointed behind him. "In front of the office building."

Hannah followed the woman's finger then caught Dale once again seeking her approval with his eyes. She nodded again and watched for a short beat as he turned on his heel and walked briskly to the exit, a slight limp in his gait. She'd forgotten about his leg and his discomfort the night they'd met. Maybe she should try getting her new *volunteer* on a horse too.

• • • •

Dale wasn't sure what to expect. Once he was within view of the car, he assessed the lone figure on the passenger side. Clean cut young man anywhere from fifteen to twenty. Unlike your average person of that age, he wasn't fidgeting with the radio or glued to his cell phone. He sat perfectly still, eyes ahead. Dale wasn't even sure he'd seen the kid blink. The closer he got to the car, Dale realized the windows were both rolled down. Good, he didn't have to worry about startling the teen by tapping on the window.

"Nice day, isn't it?" He probably could've thought of something more original, but simple usually worked best.

The passenger turned to face him. "I want to go home."

He'd faced angry kids enough times before to recognize when a really angry kid was in front of him. He also knew at this point trying to coax him out of the car would be a wasted effort. "Where's home?"

The kid didn't bother to face him again. And he was definitely still a kid, no matter what his mother thought. Dale would venture a guess of seventeen. Maybe eighteen, but if he were a legal adult, Dale would bet a year's salary the kid would not be here now. Dale was sticking with seventeen.

Almost under his breath, the teen mumbled, "Midland."

"Never been out that way. Always lived in Midland?"

The kid nodded. No help in conversation here.

"Worked with a guy once from around there. He claimed there was a desert with dunes as high as the Sahara."

No reaction.

Dale waited a short beat. "Said he'd pretend he was at the dunes to make the sandbox more tolerable."

If the kid were a dog his ears would have perked. His shoulders stiffened and his chin lifted. Dale waited a little longer and sure enough the kid turned to face him. "Sandbox? You in the military?"

"Not now."

"But you were?"

"Marines."

Straightening a little taller in his seat, the reluctant teen met his gaze for the first time.

Dale stuck his hand into the window. "Dale Brubeck. Nice to meet you."

The way the young man stared at the dangling appendage Dale thought for a serious moment that the kid wasn't going to respond. Slowly he raised his hand and shook. "Clark Hampton." Dale considered what to say next when the kid added, "Thank you for your service."

Dale nodded, pleased the harshness in Clark's demeanor seemed to be slipping away, but not sure where to go next.

"How long were you in?" the kid asked.

"Eight years."

Clark scanned Dale's arms and legs quickly, met his eyes once again. "Why'd you leave?"

"It was time." Some of his buddies were still in. Willing, some eager, to put in their twenty, but for him and DJ it had been time to go.

"You work with SEALs?" Clark kept his attention on Dale.

He supposed that was a good thing. "Some. Not often. I was an MP."

"Military police." The kid seemed to be weighing the words. Once more Dale didn't have a clue if that was a good or bad thing, but common sense told him if he still had the teen's attention, any attention had to be a good thing.

Footsteps grew louder behind Dale, and Clark's gaze shifted past him. The tension that had slowly given away during what little conversation they'd shared sprang back to life.

Mrs. Hampton and Hannah approached the car in near parade formation, the only similarity their pace and gait. Where Hannah was young and casual, and even under the mantle of responsibility, her eyes sparkled with the joy of life. Mrs. Hampton, on the other hand, looked to have fallen off the pages of a fashion magazine. Pressed slacks, expensive blouse, not a hair out of place, and her leather boots with narrow heels would be more suitable for a stroll down Fifth Avenue than crossing a Texas ranch.

"I think this will be just fine, if we can get Clark out of the car next time." The lady nodded at Hannah and quickly skirted around the front of the car without ever glancing at her son.

Hannah waited until the car was almost to the front gate before turning to face him. "Maybe I'll warm up to her."

"Or freeze." He shook his head. "The kid's angry, but reachable. Don't know what the mother's excuse is."

"Frustration. I'd hope to have a few seconds at least to talk to her son, but she moved so fast I couldn't even get in an introduction."

"We didn't really have that much time, but if I'm reading him correctly, he's impressed by the Marine Corps."

Hannah crossed her arms and cocked her head looking up at him. "A way with horses, and now a way with rebellious teens. What other surprises do you have in store for me?"

And wasn't that a loaded question?

CHAPTER TEN

The startled look on Dale's face wasn't what Hannah had expected.

"I think it's too soon to determine if I have a way with teenagers, horses, or anything else."

"You may be right about the boy, but you definitely have a way with horses." Hannah turned toward the barn. "Let's get everything wrapped up and head for the house."

"So when do the lessons start?" Dale kept in step beside her.

"Monday."

"You don't look very happy about that."

"We're pretty much ready. Insurance and other business details are in order. I still need to work on a volunteer list and a few miscellaneous loose ends. But all in all, we can make this work."

"I don't know how long I've been grounded for, but as long as I'm here, I'm willing to help." Dale chuckled. "That is, if your aunt agrees."

Hannah reached the open doorways to the pasture where Maggie and a couple other horses pranced about a fenced pasture. These animals remained indoors a good part of the day, cooped up in their stalls. Soon they would be working hard helping children and adults with their lives. Whenever possible, it was nice to just let them be horses.

"That is," she enunciated clearly, "if you know anything more about horses than how to sweet talk them."

"I'm a fast learner."

Shifting focus from the horses to the man at her left, she bit back a grin. What she wouldn't give to find the key to opening this man up and seeing what made him tick. Why was DJ willing to go out on a limb for a stranger? "I bet you are."

Startled eyes wide as saucers blinked back at her.

She couldn't help smiling at him. "Has anyone ever told you you're adorable when you're flustered?"

"I'm pretty sure neither the words flustered nor adorable are used very often in reference to me." This time Dale's startled look was replaced by a full-wattage smile that made her mind go blank.

Standing perfectly still a beat or two longer than required, she drew in the details of his face, the crinkle at the corners of his eyes when he smiled, the dimple on his left cheek, the flecks of gold in the sea of caramel. A whinny in the distance pulled her attention back to the business at hand. "It was amazing to see Maggie with you."

Dale put his foot on the bottom rung of the fence, and leaning forward, rested his forearms along the top, watching the horses in the distance. "I just talked to her."

"Well you must be fluent in equine, because any other strange male who would have tried to set foot in that stall would most likely have been catapulted into the next county."

"I find that hard to believe. She's a sweet girl."

"And you would know that how?" Hannah leaned over the fence as well. Maybe at ease like this he'd be willing to open up some more. "Have you been holding out on me? Were you raised on a horse ranch in Wyoming, or perhaps in bluegrass country?" She was only kidding, but if he admitted either of the possibilities, she wouldn't have been at all surprised.

"Nope. City boy through and through. Army brat to be more precise."

"Right. New York and Philadelphia. Where do you call home?"

"I don't." He shrugged. "I guess home is wherever I hang my hat."

For the first time since meeting him yesterday, despite the sore back, despite the scare this morning with the blood clot, only now did she feel sad for him. Maybe she was better off not knowing more. She always felt extremely lucky to have had such a strong tight knit family. There was something very special about home. As much as she loved being at Aunt Eileen and Uncle Sean's, it wasn't truly her home. And it hurt her to think Dale didn't have any place to call his.

"Don't look so serious." Fingers casually linked, he turned to stare at her. "I'm happy. King of the road."

"Ah, yes. The handsome king on his powerful iron steed, sweeping women off their feet. How could I forget?"

"You mean knocking them off their feet?" One side of his mouth tipped up in a lopsided smile. A smile that had her once again staring at his features with fascination. "I really am sorry."

"You've said that already. Apology already accepted."

He shrugged one shoulder, and the other side of his mouth tilted up for an even smile. "Are you still going to check out a horse?"

It took him a few seconds to remember the reason she'd come to Connor's in the first place. "It's getting late. I don't have time to put her through the paces."

Dale rolled his neck from side to side, stretched his shoulders, and Hannah remembered his sore back.

"But, before I bring the horses inside, it wouldn't hurt you any to show your stuff."

"Excuse me?" That flustered look took over Dale's face again.

"You heard me. Come on."

It didn't take long to have Dale in front of Patience, shaking his head. "I don't know about this. Your aunt might come after us."

"What she doesn't know won't hurt her." Hannah saddled Patience quickly and walked her in between the mounting blocks. "Just like climbing onto a motorcycle."

Dale reached for the saddle horn and hefted himself up and over with a slightly muffled groan. "Not exactly."

Leading him into the arena, they came to a stop by the first square. "I want you to warm up. Stretch your arms out and swing left then right." She took him through several simple arm swirls and movements. "Feel all warmed up now?"

"You could say that." He flashed that impish grin.

Hannah felt her cheeks warm. "Let's start walking. Patience has a lateral gait. She'll be good for those sore back muscles."

"It's not my back I'm worried about." Sparkling eyes filled with humor turned away from her.

It was in her best interest not to let her gaze wander to his rear in the saddle. "Yeah, well, no pain no gain."

"Ha ha." He didn't look at her, but she could see his smile expand nonetheless.

Not wanting to overdo it, they walked around a few more minutes before returning inside for him to dismount.

"That wasn't as bad as I expected."

"You'll feel it tomorrow, but the day after you can ride again. We'll do this till you leave. You'll be surprised how much better your muscles will feel."

Dale didn't look all that convinced, but the way he helped remove the saddle and clean Patience up, she had the feeling he was teasing her just a little.

With Patience in her stall for the night, Hannah climbed onto the bottom rung of the nearest fence, one hand at the top and the other hand to her mouth, she whistled loud and strong for Maggie.

Not far ahead the horse lifted its head, pawed at the dirt and turned away.

"Little stinker," Hannah muttered and ignored the chuckle coming from Dale. Both hands to her lips she blew out the familiar call for the horse, shifted her weight to blow one more time, and felt her balance give way. Arms flailing and letting loose a loud squeal, she moved her legs to find a foothold, only to be scooped and cradled in strong arms for the second time in two days.

"You okay?" Dark narrowed eyes filled with concern drilled her.

"Thanks to you, yes." Her words did little to ease the

concerned gaze taking her in.

Was it totally ridiculous that she had an overwhelming urge to lay her head on his shoulder, wrap her arms around his neck and stay curled in his arms till, oh, whenever? She actually had to consciously keep from pouting when one arm fell away from underneath her, letting her legs reach the ground. When she was standing steady on her own two feet, his other hand eased away and that high wattage smile reappeared. "We really should stop meeting this way."

***

Dale was thankful that Hannah was so easy to talk to. Finished brushing the horse down, putting her back in the stall, and taking the short ride back to the Farraday ranch, he'd asked her everything and anything he could think of to keep his mind off how much he had wanted to keep her in his arms.

Even now the urge to reach out and snatch her hand in his was surprisingly strong. He hadn't felt like this about a girl he barely knew since he was a teen crushing on the head cheerleader. "How old were you when you sat your first horse?"

"Too young to remember." She sprouted a cute grin that told him she remembered more than she was willing to share.

"When did you know you wanted to do equine therapy?"

The car rolled to a stop. Hannah shifted gears and popped the door open. "I'm not really sure exactly when it made sense to mix my degree with my history with horses."

"So you were already in college?" Dale climbed out of the car.

"Oh, yeah, for sure."

The front door flung open and her aunt filled the doorway. "This, I'm sure, is not what Brooks meant by take it easy."

Hannah shrugged. "I'm not a doctor. But even I know people get blood clots from laying still."

"I'm not a doctor either, and I know that people throw clots by moving around."

Dale didn't dare get in the middle of this one, even if it was about him. One thing he had learned early in life was when to stand his ground and when to take cover. Right now, diving for the nearest recliner and taking it easy as the woman wanted seemed the safest move.

Aunt Eileen ushered him into the other room. "Come on inside and let's get you settled. Brooks will be here soon, and DJ won't be far behind."

"Twice in one day is a lot for Brooks to come out here." Hannah grabbed the cushion out of the recliner and tossed it onto the sofa. "What can he do that we can't?"

Aunt Eileen stood by the chair, fists on her hips, clearly waiting for Dale to settle in, but staring down her niece. "Blood clots are a serious matter. Which is why," she turned to face Dale, "you are going to stay put until Brooks arrives."

"Yes, ma'am." Dale almost saluted before dropping into the nearby recliner.

"Good. Would you like something to drink?"

"No, ma'am. Thank you."

"All right, I've got a little more work in the kitchen. Just took a couple of pumpkin pies out of the oven."

Hannah whiffed the air. "Is Meg coming?"

"How did you know that?" Aunt Eileen asked.

"Seriously? Even I know Meg's favorite is anything pumpkin. That's the only reason I can think of you would bake a pumpkin pie out of season."

Aunt Eileen smiled at her niece, patted her cheek with one hand and kissed the other cheek. "You always were a smart kid."

"Need help in the kitchen?"

"Nope. Just make sure this guy stays put."

Hannah took a seat on the sofa closest to him. Dale chose to wait until the aunt was out of sight. "She really is something, isn't she?"

"Oh yeah. And when she and my mom get together, heaven help us all."

"Really? Two peas in a pod?"

"Two crazy peas in a pod."

He took a minute to consider that. The woman was caring, perhaps a little over the top, perhaps not. Loving, kind, a little bossy, but from love obviously. All those qualities said a lot about Aunt Eileen, but so far he hadn't read crazy. "How crazy?"

"Well," Hannah blew out a small huff, "maybe crazy isn't quite the right word. Maybe silly is better. They always break out in song. You don't want to be behind them at Wal-Mart if a song they like starts playing. They wind up dancing down the aisle and embarrassed you'll duck behind the displays."

Dale laughed at that one. So far he'd pictured Aunt Eileen more like a drill sergeant than a chorus girl.

"They tell jokes no one else gets, spit old movie quotes back and forth at each other."

"That seems rather harmless."

"In the living room of course it does, but at restaurants, grocery store, and other places where waitresses and cashiers are trying to do their job, except the two of them aren't paying attention because they're reciting word for word scenes of dialogue from movies. Whatever you do, don't ask her to recite the *What pants should I wear* scene from *My Cousin Vinny*."

Another burst of laughter escaped from deep in his chest. At least Aunt Eileen had good taste. The woman sounded like a firecracker. He really liked that—a lot.

"Of course when she gets all the friends together you'll want to hide the rifles."

Okay, that sounded more serious, teetering on dangerous, but before Dale could inquire further the front door creaked open.

"Glad to see you're still with us." Brooks came in

"Alive and kicking," he confirmed.

The door still open, Meg and Adam crossed the threshold. The redhead had barely made it into the house when, nose to the air, she sniffed like a bloodhound following a scent. "Oh please tell me that's Aunt Eileen's famous pumpkin pie I smell."

"Two of them." Hannah grinned.

Adam turned to close the door and stopped midway. "I see brother Declan has arrived."

"Looks like we're going to have a full house." The pregnant woman settled her hands on her rounded tummy.

Boot heels clattered down the wooden steps. The first person to emerge from the second floor was the family patriarch. By the time DJ made it into the house, the youngest brother Finn was descending the stairs. Brooks' wife wasn't kidding. Adding in siblings and houseguests and in-laws and cousins, this family was as big as a church. Sort of ironic. After all, churches offered sanctuary too.

CHAPTER ELEVEN

DJ had hoped for less of an audience when he got to sit down with Dale. Not wanting to accidentally set off any red flags in Dallas, he'd resisted checking into things, but he did call the hospital to follow up on his friend the same as he done every few days for the past weeks. As soon as he'd been informed that Officer Dale Johnson had died, DJ understood better some of what was going on. What he needed to figure out now was if keeping Dale here was putting his family at risk.

"Where's Becky?" Hannah asked.

"My wife and her grandmother are helping Kelly make new slipcovers. Though I'm a little concerned how much progress they're going to make."

Meg sidled up to her brother-in-law for a quick kiss on the cheek. "What makes you say that?"

"It might have something to do with the two bottles of white wine and a batch of Toni's Chardonnay cake balls." DJ smiled.

All heads turned to Toni. Patting her tummy, she grinned widely and hefted her hands in a casual shrug. "Hey, I had to do something to help liven up a Saturday night with slipcovers."

High-fiving with her sister-in-law, Meg said, "If I had the slightest clue which end of a sewing machine was up, I'd have been there to help just for the cake balls."

"Those suckers really are popular." Brooks looked to his wife. "If you ever got a bee in your bonnet to open a cake ball business, I could probably retire."

Toni patted her husband's arm lightly. "Keep dreaming, sweetie. Keep dreaming."

"I could eat the rear end of a rhinoceros at this moment." Sean Farraday looked past his sons and their wives to Aunt Eileen entering the room.

"Me, too," Hannah grinned.

The patriarch looked to Aunt Eileen. "Whatever's cooking smells delicious."

Aunt Eileen rolled her eyes at her brother-in-law. "After a long day like today, you'd say that if I were brewing leather and shoelaces."

"That's only because," Sean smiled, "your culinary skills are such that even leather and shoelaces would be delicious."

"Suck up!" two of the brothers hollered.

DJ slapped his dad on the shoulder. "What did you break?"

"Nope," Adam shook his head "my guess is he bought something."

"Lord I hope it's new boots." Aunt Eileen waved a finger. "You can only resole a pair of boots so many times."

Sean Farraday shook his head at his sons. "Fat lot this bunch knows. I didn't break anything. I didn't buy anything. And your aunt is a great cook and y'all know it."

Several heads in the room nodded at the woman now smiling from ear to ear.

"And I'd like to think," Sean pointed from son to son, "that I have taught each and every one of you to give man, or woman, credit where credit is due and praise when warranted."

His dad was right, but they all appreciated their aunt and what she'd done for them and no one minced words in this family. That left the detective in DJ a little surprised by the sternness of his father's rebuke. Then again, after twelve hours working the ranch, the man had a right to be a little grumpy.

"Well," Aunt Eileen blew out a light breath, "supper's taking a little longer tonight. I think we're going to be in the market for a new oven. Knob says 350, but I took a thermometer reading and it's fifty degrees under. Y'all might as well grab a drink. It'll be a bit longer." She spun to face DJ. "And I'd like a few minutes with you when you have a chance."

DJ swallowed and nodded. He knew what she'd want, but the

whole reason Dale said nothing to him was about to be showcased. DJ couldn't tell his aunt what he didn't know. Taking advantage of the time till supper, he turned to his friend. "Why don't you join me for a cold one on a country porch?"

"He can join you on the country porch," Brooks got to his feet, "but no cold ones."

Aunt Eileen turned to Dale. "How does some fresh squeezed strawberry lemonade sound?"

Dale's face lit up as though she'd offered him the winning lottery numbers. "Like heaven on earth, ma'am."

Adam followed Dale out the back door. Brooks remained seated by his wife. The guy might be a doctor, but when it came to Toni and her pregnancy, Brooks behaved more like a mother hen. His dad and Finn escaped to the office for a few minutes. Any paperwork done before supper meant one less thing to deal with before bed.

"Oh, man, the lemonade is out of this world." Dale practically licked his lips.

"Dad wasn't kidding," Adam spoke up. "Aunt Eileen really is great in the kitchen. She's probably the best cook in the county. Her jams and pies are always winning blue ribbons at the state fair."

"I'll make sure to leave some room for that pumpkin pie she baked."

From the way Dale eyed him over the rim of his glass, DJ knew his friend recognized he was itching for a chance to talk alone. Taking another sip, Dale scanned from left to right across the horizon. "This is a lot of land."

"Over 100,000 acres before we bought some of the Brennan land," Adam said.

Dale shifted his attention toward the barns. "Is that for cows or horses?"

DJ muffled a laugh. "Sometimes we have to keep a calf or a first-time pregnant heifer inside. But usually we keep horses in the barn."

"I'd love to take a look. Want to show me around?"

And this was why DJ had loved working with Dale. That guy could follow a breadcrumb of a hint. Together their work sang. "Sure, we have a little time."

Not until they'd crossed into the barn did Dale speak. "I appreciate what you've done. But I'm not sure this was such a great idea."

"That's what I'm about to find out."

Dale nodded and stepped further inside, pausing at the first stall to scratch the chin of a horse whose head hung over the doorway.

"I called the hospital today," DJ said. "Dale Johnson passed away two days ago."

Remaining silent, Dale continued to scratch the horse's chin with one hand, and stroked his neck with the other. "Who else did you call?" he finally asked.

"No one. It was one thing for me to check the hospital the way I've been doing all along, it was another to start poking under rocks. Never know which –"

"—snake will jump out and bite you." It was an expression they'd used often when they were partnered on the Dallas PD.

"I think I can figure a few things out for myself."

Dale turned sideways to face DJ, but continued to scratch the horse's chin.

"The different name is obvious to any idiot. If Dale is dead it wouldn't do any good to have people reporting that they've chatted with you after the funeral."

"There is no funeral. Mom flew home when I was transferred out of ICU and into a regular room. As far as anyone in Dallas is concerned, Dale Johnson was sent home to his family."

"And you're sure nobody's checking up to see that your family is burying a body?"

"Very sure."

Something in the way Dale said that struck DJ as odd. They both knew in this business no one could ever be absolutely sure of anything. "What am I missing?"

Dale's hand fell away from the horse. He blew out a heavy sigh and turned to fully face DJ. "Peter Mackinaw didn't like people. You know the kind. The ones all the fighting changes, soon the wife leaves them, the parents don't understand them, and anger and pain fester inside like a cancer."

DJ knew too damn well what he was talking about.

"I had the bed by the window, Pete had the bed by the door. Sometimes he'd shuffle over to the window and stare for hours. I offered to have the hospital switch beds on us, but he always said no. Until the other night. It was late and he'd been standing staring out the window at absolutely nothing for so long I expected him to just drop from exhaustion. This time when I said *Hey man, why don't you sleep here* and *I'll take the other bed*, he never answered. He merely turned, walked to my bed, and started to sit before I could climb fully out."

Far-off look in his eyes, Dale's mind had no doubt gone someplace very unpleasant. Whether he was thinking about Peter, or the murder-suicide he'd responded to weeks before the accident, or the accident itself, DJ had no way of knowing. But he understood nonetheless.

"I'd taken some meds for the pain and fell fast asleep. Had the craziest dream. I rolled over, opened my eyes, and saw a tall figure injecting something into Peter's IV. Then, like the Grim Reaper, the dark shadow casually strolled out of the room, closing the door behind him. I thought for sure it was a sign that my days were numbered since Peter was actually in my bed. All of a sudden machinery started beeping. Alarms were going off, nurses and doctors were running through the room. The scene looked like a cartoon football huddle. Not till I woke up at six in the morning to an empty bed beside me did I realize it was no dream."

"Damn it, man. I'm so sorry," DJ said. "You think that was meant for you?"

"I know it was. I wasn't pining over a breakup. Despite what you or anyone else might have thought, I could still compartmentalize life and work. Though it may drive me over the edge one day, it hasn't yet." Dale pushed away from the stall and took a few steps closer to DJ. "I didn't drive off the road. I was run off the road."

• • • •

"You seem awfully quiet tonight." Aunt Eileen handed Hannah another tomato to slice. "Something you want to talk about?"

"Just thinking about a new student."

"For the new riding program?"

"Yes. Looks like starting Monday, we're open for business."

Aunt Eileen wiped her hands on a dishrag. "But I thought there was a long waiting list?"

"There is for the subsidized sessions. We're still getting the funding in place for those. But I've got a paying student who starts Monday. His mother didn't want to wait for the official start in two weeks. And after hearing his story, I can't say that I blame her."

"Young boy?"

"Teen. Senior in high school. I can't say much more right now."

Aunt Eileen nodded. She knew better than anyone, sometimes life just handed out a raw deal. "Let me finish the salad. You go tell the men on the porch it's time for supper."

"DJ and Dale are in the barn. I noticed them walk off a bit ago." She didn't want to tell her aunt that she'd been watching carefully and had kept an eye out the window for their return. They'd been gone long enough for Finn to have joined Adam on the porch. "I can run out and let them know."

Her aunt broke out in a wide grin. "You do that, sweetie." Hannah was halfway out the door when her aunt shouted over her shoulder with an even bigger grin. "And you let me know if you see that dog anywhere."

She couldn't be upset with her aunt, even she'd been looking for a dog the first time she met Dale. It seemed the whole town was judging whether or not another Farraday would find their mate by if the stray dog appeared. How absurd was that? But she had to admit, it was going to make for some great storytelling to her cousin's grandkids.

On the porch she glanced toward the barn and back to her cousins. "Aunt Eileen's putting supper on the table. She wants y'all inside. I'll head over to the barn and collect DJ and Dale."

Too far away to make out the words, she'd walked close enough to the barn to hear the low rumble of the male voices and recognize the serious tone of the conversation. Curiosity had her considering what two near strangers could be discussing so seriously. She was going to have to mind her own business when it came to this particular stranger. Houseguest or not, way with horses are not, his life was none of her business. A few more days and he would be on his way again. She'd best keep reminding herself. Whether she liked it or not. Unless...

CHAPTER TWELVE

"So why in the hell was somebody running you off the road?" DJ stared at Dale as though he expected him to answer.

"I can't tell you that. The less you know—"

"Don't hand me that bullshit. This is me. We had each other's backs in the sandbox long before Dallas. I'll have your back now, but you have to tell me what the hell I'm up against."

"Even though it wasn't my first choice to hideout here, for only a couple of days everything should be fine. I bought the bike with a full tank of gas off a guy from the paper. Worked my way out of Dallas on the back roads. Avoided street cameras and tollways."

"Which is why you were hurting so bad by the time you got here. Must've taken you twice as long to get to a camera-free part of the freeway."

Dale nodded. They both knew how easy it was to be found even when somebody did their utmost to stay hidden. But he'd covered his bases. He had a decent wad of cash in his pocket thanks to his captain, the only other person besides the DA who knew the truth.

"How long are we talking?" DJ asked.

"Not too long, I hope." He considered a moment just how much he wanted to stay, but DJ was right about one thing. They'd been partners too long and in too many places to leave him completely in the cold. "The DA's putting a case together. When it's done I'll be back to testify. Then it will be over."

"You two look awfully solemn for a couple of guys out playing with the horses." Hannah stepped into the barn. The way the setting sun shined at her back, she truly looked like an angel.

"He's a Red Sox fan." DJ sprouted a scowl and flung a thumb over his shoulder at Dale. "Enough said." Without looking back, DJ left the two of them still rooted to the ground.

Frowning at her cousin's back, Hannah cocked her head to look up at Dale. "I didn't think he cared that much about baseball."

"Who knew?" Dale shrugged casually—he hoped. Truth was he really was a Red Sox fan even though he never lived anywhere near Boston. "What about you? You into sports?"

Hannah fell into step beside him. "If you're asking me am I a Red Sox fan, the answer is no. Go Rangers all the way."

"You like baseball?"

"Season tickets to the Frisco Rough Riders. Though I suppose that makes no sense now that I'm going to be living out here."

"Season tickets?" Dale tried not to gape. A woman who loved baseball enough to buy season tickets and she had to be DJ's little cousin, and at a time in his life when sticking around wasn't an option.

"Mrs. Stewart, a major donor to the equine center I used to work at, has the sweetest seats for the Texas Rangers. Her family has had them since the old stadium. Second row behind the Ranger dugout."

Dale whistled.

"I know. Mrs. Stewart had to substitute for the hostess of some big charity gala last fall. Her granddaughter was having a riding session when she got the call. I must've mentioned in our conversations that I liked baseball because she offered me four tickets for that Friday night's game. My brothers Jamie and Ian and my cousin Grace came with me." She chuckled low in her chest. "Ruined me for any other seat in the house."

"I bet." When she laughed she looked so sweet, so beautiful. And so young. Knowing he should pick up the pace to the house but preferring to amble at the slower West Texas stride, he savored this chance to spend time alone with Hannah. "So, who's your favorite player?"

"All-time favorite Ranger? No-brainer, Pudge Rodriguez."

"And now?"

Her eyes twinkled with amusement. "Beltre. The man seems to be having so much fun when he plays ball. Always teasing and laughing with players." She kicked at a stone in the path. "Listen, there's something I wanted to ask you."

He braced himself. "Okay?"

"Today, when Mrs. Hampton sent you out to talk to Clark."

Dale nodded, steeling himself for what might come next.

"Normally I like to be the first one to reach out to a new student. To connect. To evaluate. But she put us both on the spot. Given how important it was to make a good impression on her, especially if I want her friend Mrs. Stewart to help us with this new program, I didn't say anything."

"I'm sorry. I didn't mean to step on any—"

"No," she cut him off, "it wasn't your fault. And frankly I was a little surprised to see how you connected with him. I'd like to use that to my advantage maybe."

"What did you have in mind?"

"Our first session is going to be Monday morning. There's always a volunteer during a class who stands nearby in case the student needs help or if the horse has to be led."

Dale nodded again, but wasn't sure he would like the next thing she said.

"Grace is out of town in Houston on a combination fundraising public relations jaunt, and Catherine is terrified of horses. I was hoping," she looked skyward as though searching for something before glancing back at him and piercing him with her gaze, "you might be willing to step in as a volunteer with Clark."

Right now there wasn't anything he'd like more than to step in and help Hannah with anything she asked, but in a couple more days he should have the okay from Brooks to travel with only the oral medication. Sticking around any longer than necessary would not be a smart idea. And he was definitely a smart cop. But he was also a man who recognized a kid in trouble, who never could refuse a damsel in distress, and too often—his own worst enemy.

"Sure, I'd love to."

• • • •

"Here we go." Eileen set down two bowls of fresh whipped cream to go with the pumpkin pies she'd made earlier in the day.

While she cut the first slice and handed it off to their guest, DJ picked up the bowl and scooped a massive dollop over Dale's piece of pie. "You are going to want to taste this. Hand whipped from farm fresh cream."

Dale reached for his fork. "I've always had a soft spot for whipped cream."

"Tell me about it." DJ shook his head and put the bowl back in place.

There it was again. That odd hint of familiarity. More than once Eileen had thought she noticed a quiet communication that she usually only saw in married people. And she might not understand where these responses were coming from, but she was darn sure the two had never been married. Cornering her nephew before serving dinner hadn't done a dang bit of good in ebbing her curiosity. If the man had secrets, he knew how to keep them.

"Oh." Eyes closed, Toni groaned and every head in the room snapped around. "This is so good," she muttered. When she realized she was the object of everyone's attention, she rolled her eyes. "The pie, people. The pie."

"I'll have another piece please." Hannah handed off her plate.

Eileen would kill for her niece's metabolism.

"So," Dale pointed his chin at Toni. "When are you due?"

"Any day now."

"Oh." He looked from her to Brooks and back. "Guess he or she isn't in a hurry."

"First baby foot-dragging syndrome." Brooks patted his wife's hand. "They come when they're good and ready, not when we tell them."

"I'm good and ready." Toni stabbed at another bite of pie.

"Hope that counts for something."

It did Eileen's heart good to see all her boys so happy. Even Grace the baby had found a perfect match. She just wished the matchmaking dogs would bring someone nice for Hannah. Not that there was any hurry to marry her niece off. At almost twenty-six, Hannah was the youngest of all the Farradays including the cousins, but that didn't mean she couldn't have someone special in her life. Everyone deserved to share their world with someone.

Eileen looked to each of the young couples at the table, then over to her brother-in-law before gently tapping the letter in her pocket. Everyone deserved somebody.

CHAPTER THIRTEEN

Sundays were Hannah's favorite day of the week. The one day when every member of the family came together after church for supper and occasionally an extra friend or two would tag along. Having been the only one left at home in Hill Country for the last few years, she really loved the crowd. Normally, this Sunday would have been the potluck lunch at church. She'd actually been looking forward to that. But under the circumstances, with Dale at the ranch keeping a low profile and all the shenanigans with the social club yesterday, it was decided she'd stay home with their guest. The extended family wouldn't descend on the ranch for hours.

"You really could've gone to church with everyone. I don't need a babysitter." Dale dried the last of the lunch dishes.

"Same deal as yesterday. It has nothing to do with you needing a babysitter and everything to do with keeping up appearances. As far as the folks in town are concerned I'll rest again today, and tomorrow I'll be up and ready for the world."

"It's not like any of residents of Tuckers Bluff are going to know what you're really doing."

Hannah didn't even try to hold back a laugh. "You have clearly never lived in a small town."

"I've lived in a few smaller towns."

"Nope." She shook her head. "Not buying it. Anyone who truly understands a small town would know that it does not matter how far out of town we live, everybody knows everybody's business. My cousin Grace likes to say they know the date your milk carton in the fridge expires."

"Okay. Maybe the towns I've lived in weren't quite as small as this one. But I think y'all are putting a bit more intrigue in this than is necessary."

"Maybe." She shrugged. "Or maybe not. All I know is if DJ says it's best nobody knows you're here, then this is how it's going down." Her cousin was very good at what he did and she knew it. Sometimes she wondered if there was a law enforcement gene somewhere in the family. Her brother the Texas Ranger was also very good at what he did. Sometimes she wished Ian would settle into a small town like this and take on a job that dealt mostly with reckless teens and other misdemeanors, but Ian loved what he did and she had to believe with the grace of God, he could take care of himself.

Nonetheless, she wondered what in the heck was the story of this man in front of her. Who was he running from? Why was he hiding? Or was everything truly blown out of proportion the way he said?

"You're frowning again."

"Am I?" Instinctively Hannah raised her fingers to the crease between her brows.

Dale handed her the last dry dish to stow in the cabinet. "Normally when a young woman's mind wanders, I tend to think it's over a man. When someone as pretty as you frowns, if it's over a man, he has to be a blithering idiot."

"Don't you think that's a little chauvinistic?" Hannah closed the cabinet door and turned to face him. "After all, if a man's mind wanders, he's thinking about a cure for cancer, the state of the union, the championship sport scores. But if a woman's mind drifts someplace else, it has to be over a man. Rather narrow leap, don't you think?"

"My apologies. Of course you're right. So why were you frowning?" He reached out and brushed at her forehead. "You're doing it again."

"Am I?"

"What you need is a distraction." Dale bowed at the waist, then made a broad gesture toward the living room. Straightening, he extended his elbow to her. "Follow me."

She considered asking where or why, but the words were stuck in her mouth. Before she knew it, her hand was tucked neatly in his elbow and she followed him into the living room and silently watched as he grabbed a couple of the larger pillows from the sofas and tossed them onto the floor.

"Wait here please." Spinning around, he marched back into the kitchen straight to the pantry.

"What are you doing in there?" If this was supposed to make her stop frowning, it wasn't working. She was more confused than ever.

"Considering this food closet is the size of a small house, I'm figuring your aunt has everything I want."

Hannah started for the kitchen. "Tell me what you want and maybe I can help you find it."

"Nope." Dale popped his head out. "I've got it covered. Make yourself comfortable. I'll be right there."

"But if you can't find –"

His head popped out again. "Let's try this. Please make yourself comfortable in the living room."

"Well, since you asked nicely." She hid a smile. Doing as she was told, she briefly hoped he wasn't messing up her aunt's pantry, but mostly she wanted to know what was the man up to. All settled in on the floor, she could hear the drawers in the kitchen opening and closing, the contents rattling around inside. "Are you sure you don't want my help?"

"Got it covered." Another door slammed and she heard footsteps coming in her direction. "I noticed the fireplace has a gas starter."

Hannah glanced at the wooden mantle, her eyes scanning the perimeter and landing on the metal key inset in the brick wall. "Yep, it does."

In one hand Dale carried a couple of kitchen utensils. No wait, barbecue utensils. By the time he'd reached her, she realized in his other arm he carried what he'd scavenged from the pantry. He dropped onto the cushion beside her and set down a box of graham crackers, a bag of marshmallows, and a bag of chocolate candy. Leaning forward, with the flip of his wrist, he turned the chrome key and then striking a match from the top of the mantle, held it low in the fireplace. The neatly stacked logs burst into dancing flames.

Sitting back on his haunches, he grabbed one of the barbecue forks and ripping open the bag of marshmallows, skewered two fat ones before handing the makeshift toasting device to her. "Nothing cheers a person up like a chocolate covered sugar rush for dessert."

"S'mores?" She couldn't stop grinning. It had been ages since she'd been camping. Letting out a hearty laugh she accepted the extra-long fork and grinned at her cohort. "Love s'mores."

"See. No more frowns."

"No." She held the white blob over the flames, twisting and turning, and grinning as the caramel color took over. "Nothing to frown about here."

• • • •

The bright grin on Hannah's face was enough to make Dale want to belt out a hokey Broadway tune—and he couldn't sing. This entire scenario since the day he became the DA's prime witness felt other worldly, especially since landing in Farraday country. It hadn't taken long to figure out the siblings were named in alphabetical order and then Hannah explained it was due to her Aunt Helen's love of the musical *Seven Brides for Seven Brothers*. Since Hannah was born after Grace, in honor of her Aunt Helen, her mom chose a name beginning with H to continue the musical tradition. Under the circumstances, perhaps breaking into song, no matter how off key, wouldn't be so uncalled for.

"Ouch." Hannah sucked a white droplet off her finger. "I forgot how hot roasted marshmallows can be."

Dale leaned closer for a better look. A pale pink dot grew slowly darker. "We should put that under running water."

"Nonsense, it's a marshmallow burn. We got them all the time as kids by the campfires and nobody went running for cold water. I'll survive." Lifting the smooshed and melting s'more to her mouth, she paused and pulled it away, smiling at him. "But thanks for caring."

"You're welcome." Now if he could just ignore the little dollop of chocolate and marshmallow that just landed at the edge of her mouth. It was all he could do to stop from leaning forward and licking it up himself. Instead, he grabbed his fork and shoved the marshmallow onto the end with enough force to almost skewer his hand as well.

"So what made you think of s'mores?" Hannah took another bite, then licked the sweet goo from the tip of her fingers.

He really should have thought of something a little less messy, or at least that didn't involve those pretty pink lips puckering, sucking, and licking. "It was the only dessert I couldn't mess up."

"You can't cook?"

"I can cook. Well, I can grill. I serve a mean steak, pretty good chicken, no one can match my corn on the cob, and I do okay with hotdogs and hamburgers. But unless it involves scooping out cookie dough ice cream, desserts are not my specialty."

"I love cookie dough ice cream." Hannah almost bounced off the cushion. "I love cookie dough anything. Almost as much as I love s'mores"

"There are lots of brands with s'mores flavored ice cream."

"Yeah, but I'm waiting for Blue Bell to master it."

"Ah, a true diehard Texan."

"Born and bred." She lifted her chin proudly then pierced another marshmallow. "Last one. I promise.'

"It's okay," he shrugged, "they say chocolate is an antioxidant." He was enjoying sitting on the floor with her in front of the fireplace almost as if he didn't have a care in the world.

The sound of car doors slamming carried into the house. Turning his wrist, the time of day startled him. He'd have sworn they'd only been chatting and eating for a brief while. No wonder she was swearing off any more s'mores, they'd been stuffing their faces between conversations for over two hours.

"Oh my God, what a great idea!" For a woman carrying an extra load of baby front and center, Toni Farraday made a beeline for the fireplace with the agility of a much lither person, and dragged the nearest chair up close to Hannah. "May I borrow your fork?"

"Absolutely."

"Oh wow." DJ's wife followed her husband into the house and hurriedly scrambling around him, caught up with the others in front of the fireplace. "Grace is going to be really mad she wasn't here for this."

One by one all the Farraday women gathered around the hearth, a few of their husbands hovering nearby. After squealing with delight, Aunt Eileen scurried into the kitchen and back. "I knew I'd get to use these someday." She handed everybody a yard-long narrow utensil reminiscent of a fondue fork.

Slipping his phone into his pocket, Connor was the last to enter the house. Taking a moment to scan the room, he zeroed in on Hannah. "I have a feeling things are about to really start hopping." Leaning over to help his daughter Stacey hold the marshmallow skewer higher in the fireplace, he looked to his cousin. "Apparently Mrs. Hampton likes to talk. I don't know what you said to her yesterday, but without her son having a single class with you, she is already spreading the word that you come highly recommended by Mrs. Stewart and should be an excellent replacement for the equine instructor who moved to California."

Hannah picked at some crumbs on her lap. She looked adorable casually nibbling on the dropped graham crackers. Any minute now Dale expected her to give in and make herself another S'more.

"That's a good thing," she muttered, sucking the crumbs off her finger. "Why do you look like there's too much starch in your shorts?"

"Because one of the women who also used that instructor

wants you to work with her daughter."

"Another good thing. More paying customers. Or does this person need subsidizing as well?"

A fresh s'more in his hand, Connor shook his head and took a quick bite before answering. "Paying customer."

"My favorite kind." She beamed.

"Only this paying customer wants to start tomorrow."

Hannah's exuberance for the moment fell away. "Tomorrow?"

"She's visiting her parents in Abilene for a few weeks and wants to take advantage of the closer proximity."

"You know," Catherine leaned forward on her knees, "equipment-wise, we're ready to go. There's no real reason not to take on both of these clients starting tomorrow."

Hannah looked to her cousin.

"It's up to you." Connor shrugged.

"This girl has cognitive issues and her mother fears she's regressing without the interaction with horses," Catherine said.

Dale could almost see the gears moving in Hannah's head. She was going to make this happen. And to his own surprise, he was more than pleased he'd be a part of it.

• • • •

Trying to get Dale away from the others long enough to get the rest of the story out of him had proved harder than DJ had expected. Originally he had planned to leave the church picnic ahead of the others in order to be first at home. When Sister and Sissy cornered him outside their boutique to carry on about how much fun they had at the wedding and how they could hardly wait for the next celebration, he knew he was in trouble. Then when they proceeded to prattle on for ten more minutes wanting to gab about not one, but two dogs playing matchmaker in Tuckers Bluff, he knew any chance of getting home before the rest of the family was shot to hell.

When Brooks insisted on taking Dale upstairs for a quick checkup, DJ saw his chance and ran with it. Slipping away while everybody else kept busy fixing after dinner drinks and setting up board games or chat sessions, he quietly followed his brother and friend upstairs.

"I was wondering how long it was going to take you to corner me." Dale sat down on the bed, ignoring the bewildered look on Brooks' face.

"Longer than I'd planned." DJ turned to his brother. "I hate to do this, but why don't you go wash your hands in the bathroom or something."

Brooks looked at his watch. "I'll give you fifteen minutes."

The moment the door closed, DJ turned to his friend. "You said the DA was trying to build a case."

"That's right." Dale took a seat on the bed.

"How are you communicating?"

"I have a burner cell I picked up in Tyler on my way out of town. I check in with her every few days."

"Tyler? That's a couple of hours east of Dallas. Talk about a detour to West Texas."

Nodding, Dale smiled. "If for any reason somebody picks up that I'm alive and have left Dallas, I made sure they believe I'm heading east."

"I should've known." DJ muttered. Dale had a mind as sharp as a tack and could think three steps ahead of the bad guy. "Why don't we start at the beginning?"

"We only have fifteen minutes." He turned his wrist. "Probably fourteen by now."

"Let's not waste any of it." DJ leaned against the dresser, crossed his arms and waited.

"I still don't think this is a good idea. The less you know…"

"We're not taking that route again, are we? Just tell me the truth please, and make it quick."

"All right, you win. But I want it on the record that this is under protest."

DJ nodded.

"The whole thing started a few months back, maybe longer, right after I broke up with Grace's roommate. Stopped at a restaurant near the University for a drink, sat at the bar. I had a beer, maybe two, when a woman screamed and a ruckus formed around the table behind me. You know how it is, instinct kicks in and before you know it you're right in the thick of things. Turned out to be fairly simple. Some moron screamed a man was having a heart attack. Another person yelled for CPR. But it was obvious the way the victim couldn't speak that he was choking on something. Took a quick glance at his plate as I positioned myself behind him and saw he'd ordered pork chops for dinner."

"Choked on the bone." DJ hadn't meant it as a question.

"Yep. Serves the guy right for not using a knife and fork. Anyhow, after I dislodged the thing from his throat, this character turns around and shakes my hand so vigorously he almost dislocated my shoulder. Something about him looked incredibly familiar, but with the beers and the adrenaline rush and all the people around, I didn't put my finger on it right away. He insisted I join them, ordered me another drink and asked if I'd had dinner. I hadn't, so the next thing I knew I had the biggest damn steak in front of me that I'd ever seen in my entire life."

"Times going by fast. Can we cut to the chase, please?"

"As soon as I sat down, I recognized the face. Joe Bettina."

DJ was pretty sure his eyes had popped out of his head. "*The* Joe Bettina?"

"The one and only. I had a knock on my door at 6 o'clock the next morning. By 7 o'clock, as far as Bettina and his mob were concerned, my name was Dale Henderson, salesman extraordinaire."

"You went undercover with the Famiglia Crime Organization?" DJ almost couldn't spit the words out. This was some serious crap.

"Not really. Just being chummy. Casual. Eventually I'm sure it would have gone deeper, but so far I'd simply made myself available for the occasional card game or late night drink. One day we played golf. I'm not about to tell you who made up the foursome."

This time DJ agreed. He didn't want to know. "Keep going."

"The turning point came when I got invited to Joseph's daughter's birthday celebration. At his house. On my way to the bathroom, I turned left somewhere instead of right. Found myself to one side of a slightly open door and eavesdropping with a limited view of Joe standing with his back to me and another guy across from him. In case they weren't discussing the weather, I pulled out my phone and turned on the video, but by the time I'd shifted angles for a better view, it was too late. Joe had put a bullet in the back of someone's head. He whipped around to the guy across from him, waving the gun and shouted, *that's the way you do it*, then he spun around to his other side and growled, a*re you happy now? It's done. Just the way you wanted.* Whoever gave the order responded in a language that wasn't Spanish before tossing Joe a coin. I caught one word, *Dobro*."

"Russian?" The hair on the back of DJ's neck bristled. Dealing with the mob was never a good thing, but some had no mercy, no honor code among thieves, and the Russians were one of them."

Dale waved his arms and shrugged. "Maybe. Could be any of the Slavic countries where *Dobro* means good."

"Well at least we can be sure he wasn't referring to a guitar." DJ blew out a sigh. "What did the guy look like? Were you able to make him?"

"No." Dale shook his head, his fingertips running across his left temple. "I didn't see a damn thing. I barely heard the voice, it was low and rough and hard to hear. The recorder got it, though. DA has it."

"Would you recognize it if you heard it again?"

"Yeah, I think so."

Even DJ felt a headache coming on. "So you're the reason Joe Bettina is in jail?"

Dale nodded.

"And let me guess, there's a leak in the department and your cover was blown."

Tapping the tip of his nose with his finger, Dale nodded. "That's when I found myself coming around the curve on an empty street with no brakes and a dark sedan riding my ass. Next thing I know I'm waking up in ICU with enough wires and tubes sticking out of me for a high school science experiment."

DJ needed air. He stood and walked across the room. The bedroom door inched open. Brooks popped his head in, took one look at DJ and Dale, and whispered "Ten more minutes" then closed the door behind him.

"You see my dilemma," Dale sighed. "I could've stayed at a safe house in Dallas, but my gut said *hell no*. With only two people knowing I'm alive and zero people knowing where I am—"

"One person," DJ smiled.

Dale scoffed but smiled. "Okay one. On my own I like my survival odds a whole lot better."

"Agreed." There were only a handful of people in this world outside his family DJ would trust with his life. Dale was one of them. Hand rubbing the back of his neck, DJ doubled back toward the bed. "All we have to do is get you on the stand in one piece. But without the kingpin, you'll never have a day's rest. WITSEC?"

"That's pretty much it in a nutshell."

"Does the DA have any new leads on who this person is?"

"Oh come on. Long before either of us had been on the force, these guys have had their fingers in everything from counterfeit money to identity theft, prostitution, gun smuggling, and whatever else rolls in the big bucks. Still, not once has anyone been able to find a clue or turn a perp to uncover who the top man is. We get as high as Joe Bettina and then all the leads run dry."

Shaking his head, DJ sat down again. Now he really had something to think about. Dale may have been right. Bringing him here might be the worst thing DJ could've done for the Farradays.

CHAPTER FOURTEEN

Even though Hannah wasn't working the ranch today, she and Dale rose with the rest of the family for an early breakfast.

The equipment had been left out in the arena from yesterday. She would take her new student through the paces and see where they were at.

"Where do we start?" Dale asked.

Hannah came to a stop in front of Patience's stall. "Even though you and Maggie got along like a house on fire yesterday, I'd rather not take any chances with a new student around. I read the paperwork the mother filled out for us and the history she submitted from the previous equine center, but I don't know what I'll be dealing with until I work with her. Since we don't have a mechanical horse to do an initial assessment with, it has to be on a real animal and I don't need to be worrying about the horse too."

"Makes sense. So now what?"

"We're going to get Patience saddled and ready for when Melody gets here. Just like we started to do with Maggie yesterday." Once again, with Dale at her side, she gathered up what was needed to prep the horse. "When we're done, I'll leave you with the mare while I go greet Melody and her mother."

"You alone. Got it."

"Thank you. Once we're ready, you can walk Patience over to the mounting blocks. Depending on her size and skill we'll determine how she mounts. At least we know she's not in a wheelchair and won't need the ramp."

Dale nodded. "And after that?"

"You stay nearby. You'll walk alongside Melody and the horse. If necessary you will hold the lead, but from what I understand so far, she's able to do this on her own. At some point I need you to step in to assist Melody or to take the lead for something new. Either way, I'll let you know what's going on."

"Sounds simple enough."

"It should be. We're not training for the Olympics here or gunning for a barrel racing championship. This is all about mastering the horse, building a feeling of success in kids who rarely feel they can succeed at anything in a normal world. We'll move slow and easy." She didn't feel she needed to explain anything more. The concept really was quite simple. Though she'd never gotten a straight answer these last two days of what he'd done recently for a living, it was obvious he was very bright and adaptable.

Wearing her own helmet, Melody walked in beside her mother. The girl's face broke into a smile as soon as she caught a glimpse of the horses in the stalls to the side.

Gesturing for Dale to go get Patience, Hannah extended her hand to Melody's mother. "I'm Hannah Farraday, nice to meet you." She turned to face Melody. "Thank you for coming to visit us."

"I like horses. Miss Jennifer moved away." Melody stood at about five foot four and looked like any other girl in her early teens. Her face scrunched in a frown. "I don't like Mr. John. He has a mean voice."

Hannah glanced over the girl's shoulder to the mother, looking for some affirmation. Melody's mother merely shrugged. Hannah could only take that to mean Mr. John wasn't a good fit for a teenage girl. "I hope I don't sound mean."

Melody shook her head vehemently. "You have a pretty voice, like Miss Jennifer."

"Thank you." The sound of hooves clomping on the concrete floor drew everyone's attention to Dale and Patience. "I'm going to introduce you to Patience. She's a sweet girl too. And she likes girls your age."

Grinning, Melody approached the horse with ease from the

front side. She removed a treat from her pocket and held her hand out stiff for the horse to nibble. Then taking another moment to rub the side of the horse's neck, she turned to face Hannah and proudly announced, "I like her too."

Without a word of instruction Melody turned away and walked to her place on the mounting blocks, patiently waiting for Dale to bring the horse beside it.

"We," Melody's mother started, "had been training for the horse show in Houston the end of next month. We're hoping we'll still be able to do that out of this stable."

Hannah hadn't considered getting involved in any of the events or competitions that some local cities held for horsemanship so soon. But the way Melody gleefully nodded at her as her mother spoke, Hannah didn't have the heart to say anything but, "I'm sure we can work something out."

It seems flying by the seat of Hannah's pants was becoming a regular thing for her.

● ● ● ●

Dale stood near Patience and Melody as Hannah walked them through the paces. So far he hadn't been needed to do anything, but watching Hannah work had been fascinating. Her youthful appearance completely belied the training and expertise she exhibited working with this sweet young teen. Hannah's gaze held a seriousness, a glimmer of understanding that told of a person who had seen a harsher side of life and was willing to do something about it. Sort of a kindred spirit. He and she both wanted to make a difference. He may have been too distracted to notice before, but Hannah Farraday was definitely all woman.

"That's it, now turn in the box."

The horse began to slowly step backwards.

"Where are your hands?" Hannah asked softly.

Melody lifted her hands to show Hannah and the horse took another step back.

"Yes." Even though Hannah smiled at the young girl, Dale got the feeling that was not the response she had wanted. "What do you do with your hands to stop the horse?"

Melody pulled on the reins.

"That's right, and what do you do to the reins if you want her to move forward?"

Without hesitation, Melody loosened her hold on the reins.

"Very good. That's right."

So mesmerized with the delicacy of Hannah's interaction with this honestly sweet young girl, he missed when she said for them to move across the arena for another obstacle course. "Sorry," he mumbled softly for only Hannah to hear.

With a soft smile, she gave him a slight nod. The woman embodied peace and tranquility. She was most definitely made for this job. Now he understood where her reputation had come from.

For another twenty minutes he stood beside the horse, not too far, not too close, and watched in awe as Melody worked her different skill sets and Hannah coaxed her through what would lose her points and what was more important to remember. Melody did exactly as she was told with as much intensity as any other rider might have displayed. For a moment he thought he might have a sliver of understanding of the sense of accomplishment, the confidence, improved self-esteem, that would come from handling one of these beautiful animals.

The session over, Hannah and Melody's mother spoke outside the arena while Dale walked the horse back to her stall.

Catherine came hurrying in from outside. "Sorry, crazy morning. Is the first student done?"

"Yes." Dale undid the straps under the horse and noticed Catherine take a step back. He'd almost forgotten that Hannah had told him Catherine was uneasy around the large animals.

Catherine glanced over her shoulder and back. "How did it go?"

"I'm no expert, but it seemed to go really well." He lifted the saddle off the horse and set it down on a nearby railing. "Such a sweet kid and such a shame she'll never really grow up."

"Don't write her off," Catherine came a step closer, "she's still capable of living a productive life, and probably a lot happier than the rest of us who are cognizant of all the crap in this world."

Dale nodded. "And what Hannah did in there with her is going to be a big part of it."

"Possibly." Catherine smiled.

Slipping the halter off the horse's head, then hanging it on a nearby hook, Dale turned to face Catherine. "It was amazing to see. I've watched lots of people negotiate in my time. Seen them talk someone off the ledge, both literal and mental. But it was fascinating to see her work."

"When Connor and I first considered attaching a facility for equine therapy to the new stables, we drove out to one of the best equine therapy places in Dallas. We got a chance to watch Hannah work for hours with several students. We walked away feeling the same way you do right now. We couldn't have been happier when she agreed to leave her career in the city behind to come live and work out here. We're more than fortunate to have her. We're truly blessed. Not only is she an outstanding equine instructor, she is also a licensed therapist which is really important in a small operation like ours."

"What's the difference?"

"The goal of equine therapy, or adaptive riding, as it's more commonly referred to now, is to strengthen people physically, emotionally, mentally, any one or all three through horseback riding. The instructors who work with special needs are very good at what they do, but not always prepared for what the proper response is if a student has an emotional breakdown. Whether it's because of a major accomplishment, or because of a sense of failure, or just because that's where they're at. The best stables always have a separate licensed therapist on staff."

"And you have Hannah."

Grinning like a newly engaged bride with a rock the size of Gibraltar on her left hand, Catherine nodded. "And we have

Hannah." She patted Dale on the arm and cocked her head towards the chatter at the end of the hall. "I'd better get to the office and see where we stand now with our new student."

Near the main office, Hannah shook Melody and her mother's hands as Catherine stepped in to escort them to the front of the building.

He should've continued doing what he knew to unsaddle the horse, but he couldn't stop himself from watching Hannah walk toward him.

The way her eyes shone, he could tell she was pleased with the session. "Need some help there, cowboy?"

"Cowboy? I've been called a lot of things in my day, but cowboy has never been one of them."

She reached into the bucket and grabbed a brush before coming to a stop in front of him. "You keep handling the horses like that, you're going to earn that title." Her arm brushed against his as she stepped closer to Patience, and softly praising the horse, began brushing her down.

Grabbing another brush from the same bucket, he stepped around to the horse's other side and mimicked her strokes, laughing to himself. *Cowboy.* Like he could ever fit in to this simple way of life.

CHAPTER FIFTEEN

Soaring on an adrenaline high, Hannah was surprised her feet were still touching the ground. She adored when she could connect with one of her students, but today was especially sweet, the first official session at Capaill Stables.

"I don't know about you, but I am starved." Dale latched the stall gate behind them. "How much time do we have before Clark gets here?"

"Not till later this afternoon. I wish I could take you into town. Frank at the café makes homemade biscuits twice a day and right about now I've got a hankering for those babies with fresh butter and Mrs. Cheney's honey."

"Not fair, you have my mouthwatering."

The two pulled into the drive a car length ahead of Finn, who'd done a run into town for supplies. With Joanna in Dallas doing the final wedding prep with her mom, he'd had a hard time keeping busy. It was funny seeing the change in him since his fiancée came into his life again. The quiet, serious one of the family was now always smiling and rarely quiet. And most definitely happier than a pig in slop.

"Here." Aunt Eileen waved from the kitchen. "I thought you'd barely have time to sneak away for lunch today."

"Are you kidding? I'm starved." Hannah went straight to the oven and turned on the light to peek inside.

"That's zucchini bread." Aunt Eileen pointed to the oven. "Miss Cheney dropped off a bag of zucchini with her honey this morning. She accidentally planted twice as much as usual and now she has a bumper crop."

Finn came into the kitchen and kissed his aunt on the cheek. "Well, if that puts us on the receiving end of your zucchini bread, I won't complain."

"It's also going to have you on the receiving end of zucchini tots, zucchini fries, and zucchini hash browns. I've also been marinating some sliced zucchini. Thought tonight you and your dad could grill some with the rib-eyes."

"Works for me." Finn poured himself a glass of ice water.

"Me too." Hannah loved vegetables that didn't taste like vegetables. Even though the zucchini fries weren't the same as French fries, they were still pretty darn good, and the zucchini tots are better than tater tots. Her aunt did the same thing with cauliflower. For the longest time as kids they didn't even realize they were eating vegetables.

Finn's cell phone rang and his face lit up. "I'll take this in the office."

"Judging from that grin plastered on his face, that has to be Joanna." Aunt Eileen pulled the bread out of the oven, and setting it on a cooling rack, shoved a couple of other trays into the oven. "Which means we won't see him for a good half hour."

"I'll set the table." Hannah opened a kitchen drawer to collect silverware.

"Set extra places for Connor and Catherine. They're going to join us." Aunt Eileen turned to face Dale. "Would you mind heading over to the barn and letting Sean know that we'll be having lunch in about twenty minutes. He'll want to come in and wash up first."

"My pleasure." Dale flashed a sweet grin, dipped his chin, and turned to do as he was told.

Aunt Eileen stared after him for a few seconds before turning her attention back to the stove. "He seems like such a nice fellow. But have you noticed he doesn't talk much about himself?"

"Some." What Hannah had noticed was that she didn't have any idea what he did for a living, where he lived, where he came from, or where he was going. And yet oddly enough she felt as though she knew so much about him.

"Has he said where he's from?"

At least she could sort of answer to this one. "He's not really from anywhere. He's an Army brat, and you already know a Marine."

"Yes. That explains a few things."

Hannah looked up from the table. "Like what?"

"For one thing, why he and DJ seemed to hit it off as if they were old friends."

"DJ hits it off with everybody, no matter what they do."

Aunt Eileen shrugged. "I suppose."

"Do you have a problem with Dale?"

"Actually, quite the opposite. There's something solid about him. Feels like he fits right in."

Hannah didn't have to be hit over the head to know where this was going. "Just remember, once the blood thinners Brooks prescribed have kicked in, our guest will be on his merry way."

"I know that."

So did Hannah. She just needed to remind herself a few more times a day for the next few days.

• • • •

Halfway to the barn, Dale heard a rustle in a thatch of low shrubs ahead. For a split second he wondered if he was going to come face-to-face with the West Texas snake. Before he could take evasive action, the greenery moved again and a small fluff ball pranced straight for him. Squatting down, Dale extended his hand palm up. The little fur ball yipped, then rolled over on its back for Dale to rub his tummy. "Well, aren't you a cute little thing."

Usually when there was one puppy this small, there were more, but taking a quick glance around him, Dale didn't see any signs of more puppies. "I guess your brothers and sisters must be with your mom." Off the side of the barn he could see the empty dog run. He knew enough about cattle ranching to know a good cattle dog was worth two men and often a rancher would want a puppy or two to keep the bloodline going. This pup probably came from great stock. If Dale didn't know this was one of the Faradays' dogs, he'd have sworn the pup had some wolf in him.

Remembering he had been tasked with notifying Sean of lunch time, Dale reluctantly pushed to his feet. "We'll have to try this again later, little boy."

The puppy rolled over onto its feet and nodded as though answering, and made Dale laugh. If they started out this smart when they were young, no wonder a good dog was worth two men. The puppy gave a soft bark and turned to run in the opposite direction when Dale noticed Mama sitting, observing, not too far in the distance.

"Well, where did you come from?"

Mama dog stood up and nudged the little dog as it reached her feet. The puppy seemed to nod at his mom and then Mama met Dale's gaze before turning toward the rear of the barn.

"Guess your housing is on the backside," Dale muttered out loud. He was going to have to check Mama and the rest of the puppies out later today. Maybe after supper.

Sean Farraday appeared on the path. "Were you looking for me?"

"As a matter of fact, I was. Aunt Eileen sent me to fetch you. Said you'd want to know lunch will be ready in, well by now, probably fifteen minutes."

"Oh, she's running earlier than I expected." Sean fell into step beside Dale on the return path to the house.

"That may be our fault. Hannah and I came back to the ranch after her morning session."

"So how did her first official session go?"

"Everyone seemed very happy. And the young girl has a standing appointment now so…"

"All is good. And how are you feeling?"

"I feel great. But then again, I felt great before I mimicked a rug on Meg's kitchen floor."

"Too often it takes something drastic, perhaps even life-threatening, to make us see what's in front of our own noses. The way I hear it, had you collapsed anyplace else in any other time, you might not be here right now."

Dale swallowed hard. That was a difficult reality to accept. But it was what it was, and not something he was about to mess with. The whole point of hiding out was to save his life. He wasn't about to let a rogue blood clot get the better of him. Like it or not he would do exactly as Brooks said. And as fate had it, he liked following orders in West Texas way more than he thought he would.

Connor and Catherine came in the front door at the same time Sean and Dale entered from the rear and Finn emerged from his office. It was almost as if the smell of food was a siren's song for everyone. The din of chatter and bodies moving about with dishes handed over and set on the table reminded Dale more of a holiday feast than a weekday lunch. The huge platter of fried chicken was enough to have Dale drooling.

"Before someone accuses me of trying to clog your arteries, these are baked sweet potato fries." Aunt Eileen handed Dale a large bowl to place on the table of one of his favorite foods. "Finn, dear, the biscuits should be ready. Would you please pull them out of the oven?"

"You bet."

By the time everyone had taken a seat around the large kitchen table, there was enough food to have supplied his entire platoon back in the day.

"Since I had a little breakfast sausage left over, I made gravy." Aunt Eileen pilfered the biggest biscuit and poured a healthy dose of gravy over the top.

"I'm going to have to do extra time on the treadmill." Catherine blew out a resigned sigh and smiling, reached for the gravy. "But there is no way I am not having some of your biscuits and gravy."

Connor broke open a steaming biscuit and looked to Hannah. "Catherine tells me that you're considering the Houston horse show and competitions for Melody."

"I haven't had much time to think about it. But it's something she's been looking forward to and it would be a shame to disappoint her if we don't have to."

Connor dipped his biscuit in his wife's gravy, took a small bite, and grinned like a loon at her territorial glare. "I actually think it could be very good for a few reasons, but I have an idea that I'd like to run past you."

"Shoot." Hannah bit into a fry.

"What if we put together a small pre-Houston barbecue competition of our own on a much smaller scale to give Melody a little exposure?"

Hannah put the half-eaten French fry back on her plate and stared intently at Connor. Dale could almost see the wheels turning, pieces of some unknown puzzle coming together in her mind.

The crease in Hannah's brow lifted and she nodded. "That may be a fantastic idea. Last night I read up on the paperwork that Mrs. Hampton forwarded. According to her son's file, he's a senior in high school and until the accident he was the star football player."

"Which," Catherine interjected, "could explain some of that stubborn anger thing going on."

"Some of it," Hannah agreed. "He was also accepted into Annapolis. He has a lot to be angry and frustrated about."

Dale set his fork on his plate. "That explains his interest in my Marine Corps history, and why he asked if I knew any SEALs." Now things made a lot more sense. "How long ago was the accident?"

"About a year."

"Car accident?" Catherine asked softly, some of the color draining from her cheeks.

Hannah shook her head. "Oil rig. His dad's an engineer with an oil company in Midland. Clark went with him to one of the rigs. I'm not sure exactly what happened but some piece of equipment crushed his foot. They had to amputate above the ankle."

Now Dale really understood. He had more than a few friends who had lost a body part on active duty. Some handled it better than others, but it wasn't easy for any of them. "I hate to ask this but how is horse riding going to help him?"

"A few ways. He has to learn to work with the horse, he has to care for the horse, and he'll have to put something before himself. Before working with his last instructor he'd refused traditional physical therapy. A rider on horseback uses his legs to talk to a horse, to direct the horse. And as I explained before upper body strength can be built up unconsciously by balancing on a horse. Depending on the horse's movement, if it's lateral, anterior, posterior movement, etc, they all work to build different muscles."

The more Dale thought about it, he had a few friends who could probably benefit from a program like the one Connor, his wife, Hannah and her cousin Grace were putting together.

"Anyhow," Hannah continued, "Clark was an athlete, and supposedly a good one. He has to have a competitive nature."

"So he'll eat up working for a competitive goal?" Dale said.

"And," Catherine joined in, "not only could this be great motivation for a difficult student, we can use it to invite the town and locals to come see up close what we're all about."

Everyone at the table nodded. For a few seconds, Dale thought one of them was going to spring up and suggest they put on a show in the barn. He'd definitely watched too many old musicals growing up, but sometimes this family seemed too good to be true. His gaze fell on Hannah, her cheeks pink with excitement. And some people were too good to be true.

CHAPTER SIXTEEN

P ractically bursting at the seams with the thought of an event that would really pique Clark's interest, Hannah prayed he'd react the way she hoped.

"You ready?" Dale asked. "You look ready to pop."

"It shows?"

"Your enthusiasm? Hell yes." His gaze softened. "It's pretty cool how much you care about these kids, and you barely know them. Actually, you don't know Clark at all."

How could she explain? "It's the ultimate high. Sharing something I know that somebody else needs and watching them move to a better place because of it. Does that make any sense?"

"It makes a lot of sense. It's why your cousin is a cop and the other a doctor and the other a veterinarian, why your brother is a Texas Ranger, and even why your other brother is a bartender. They all help people in one way or another."

From where they stood in front of the tack room, the sound of a car door slamming shut carried easily.

"I bet that's them." Hannah shifted for a view out the front doors. "It would probably be too much if I went out there and met them, wouldn't it?"

Dale chuckled. "I don't see how it would hurt. It beats bouncing off the walls, waiting for them to come in. Let's go."

Fueled by her eagerness to share her news with Clark, her enthusiasm waned quickly at the site of Mrs. Hampton standing at the passenger door arguing with her son. "Uh oh."

"Clark William Hampton, we did not drive all the way out here for you to sit in the car. Your father made it very clear. Either we do this or you get shipped off to that therapy hospital. But you cannot spend the rest of your life sitting in a closed room."

Taking in a deep breath, Hannah blew it out slowly and put on her all-is-well-I-didn't-hear-a-thing face. "Good afternoon."

Something told Hannah the only reason Clark even glanced in her direction was a testament to what had once upon a time been good upbringing. Even angry, frustrated, and here sort of against his will, he couldn't completely ignore her. "I don't see what's good about it."

The one hope she clung to was that a small part of him must have wanted to be here, must have wanted to improve, or he wouldn't have gotten in the car in the first place. Some things were better off ignored. "Patience is all ready to give you a ride today. She's my personal horse. Brought her here from my family's ranch in Hill Country. I think you'll like her."

Clark looked from Hannah to his mother and back. "Let's go home. This is stupid."

"The only way to find out is to give it a try." Hannah tapped lightly on the car door and took a step back. "Come with me and let's give the horse a test run."

"I want to go home."

Clearly coaxing him wasn't going to get her any further than it had gotten his mother. Now she was especially glad to have the championship carrot of the Houston horse show to wave in front of him. "It's my understanding you have the fine motor skills of an athlete."

That remark earned her a dirty look.

"I could use a good horseman on our team." As she'd hoped, his gaze met hers with the last word. "This will be the first competition for our stables and it would be fun to come home a champion." Now she had his full attention. "If you'd like to come in I can tell you more about it." He didn't move. "Of course, if you want to go home…" She let her words hang and said a silent prayer.

The way his gaze skipped from the car door to the front of the office, she thought for sure he was going to accept the challenge and come inside, until she saw the exact moment his fear triumphed over his curiosity. "I want to go home."

"Officer on deck!" Dale shouted from behind her. The sound was so gruff, she actually took a step back. "Miss Farraday is the high man on the totem pole around here. She deserves the respect due an officer."

Clark stared at him. The only sign she had that he'd even heard was the muscle tick at his jaw line.

Damn, Dale. Shifting left to cut him off, she was all set to undo the damage when Dale repositioned himself in front of Clark.

"Did you hear me, midshipman?"

Clark's eyes popped. "I'm not—"

"I don't want excuses," Dale roared. "Either you have the heart of a warrior or you didn't deserve the honor of attending Annapolis. On your feet. Now!"

Hannah almost stopped breathing when Dale ordered Clark on his feet. Of all the...She didn't know where to turn to first. She could see Mrs. Hampton bug-eyed on her left and Dale, arms crossed and breathing fire, to her right. What she almost missed was Clark pushing the door open and the rubber-clad bottom tip of a crutch easing out.

Mrs. Hampton must have been as surprised as Hannah the way her jaw nearly hit the floor.

"Sir, yes, sir." Clark stood stiffly in front of Dale, the effort at balancing himself on the crutches obvious.

For a second she thought she saw a flash of concern, or perhaps remorse, spark in Dale's eyes, but just as quickly the growling drill sergeant was back. "We don't have all day."

Clark nodded and swung forward on the crutch.

"I didn't hear you," Dale bellowed.

Stunned, it took everyone a moment to follow the thread of the comment, including Clark. He figured it out a beat before she did. "Yes, sir."

"And..." Dale urged.

Another second of confusion passed and Clark turned to Hannah. "Yes, ma'am. Sorry, ma'am."

Single file, Clark led the parade to the arena. She followed after Dale, literally biting her tongue. What the hell just happened?

• • • •

Keeping a careful eye on Clark's center of gravity, Dale was far enough back to give the kid space and yet close enough to step up if he lost his footing. He could also feel Hannah's eyes drilling an angry hole in his back. He might find himself on the road out of town sooner than his doctor expected.

"Have a seat while we get Patience." Hannah gestured to a line of chairs along the wall at the head of the stalls. "It will only take a minute."

"I'll get her." Dale took one step when he spotted the sharp glare Hannah tossed his way and cut a wide berth to his right. He had a feeling the next hour might very well be the longest of his life.

From what Mrs. Hampton mentioned, Clark had been fitted for a prosthetic but refused to wear it. It was almost as if the kid was trying to sabotage his own recovery. Then again, he *was* only a kid.

The horse ready and Clark in the saddle, Hannah unbuckled a strap. "Let's tighten your girth. There. Are you ready?"

Clark gave a curt nod and then quickly looking over his shoulder to Dale, spun back to Hannah. "Yes, ma'am."

Kid was a fast learner, but if the icy glare Hannah shot Dale's way was any indication, she wasn't impressed.

"Okay, tell Patience to walk on."

The student did as he was told and the horse proceeded out of the mounting block and into the arena, Dale to one side of the horse, Hannah at the other.

Settled by the large square to the south side of the arena, Hannah stepped back. "What do you like to do to warm up?"

Dale stood aside while the young man rolled his arms as well as a few other exercises much like what he'd done the other day.

Except he could see Hannah evaluating Clark's strength and skills.

"All right, what would you like to do today?"

For most of the next hour Clark went from one exercise to another, showing off his strengths and weaknesses. Hannah's face was unreadable, though she showered the young man with praise. Pretty much every exercise was followed by "good, well done, excellent, looking good." After the hour, he had hoped to see a more enthusiastic participant, but frankly the kid's expression held the same blank angry stare, though he did see a hint of regret when it was time to dismount. Maybe there was hope.

For the last few minutes of the session, Catherine had stood on the other side of the gate watching. While Dale took the horse back to his stall to remove the saddle, Catherine and Hannah escorted their newest student out of the building. Dale hadn't gotten very far when he could hear the excited chatter of the two women returning.

"This is going to be so exciting," Catherine said.

"Now you know why I do it."

"Yeah. I felt it before. But now it all seems so very real. There is a heady rush that comes with winning an important case. With doing the right thing for someone who can't defend themselves. I always thought nothing could top that. Now I'm not so sure."

"All I know is I can't imagine myself doing anything else."

"Amen sister." Catherine gave Hannah a big hug. "I better get to work if we are going to set this thing up in only a few weeks. Wait till Grace gets back and finds out all the work we'll have piled up for her."

To Dale's surprise Hannah entered the stall and standing on the opposite side of the horse, worked with him to take care of Patience. He hadn't expected to get off the hook so easily. He'd been bracing for a major tongue thrashing. Though everything she had done until now displayed nothing but a sweet, pleasant woman, the fire in those glares told him all hell would break loose when she was angry. And right now he thought she was pretty angry. But then again, understanding women was never a man's gift. Maybe he'd gotten it all wrong.

They worked in silence until they were all done. Hannah walked Patience to the barn doors and with a slap on her rump sent the animal off to play in the fields.

The stomp in Hannah's step as they walked through the stable and turned to exit the building made it clear to anybody watching that she was not happy. On the other hand, she was a therapist, so maybe that made her one of those who stewed on her anger until she'd sorted her own feelings out and then would talk about things in a calm and rational way.

The office doors closed shut behind her. They'd made it all the way to the side of the truck when Hannah spun about with the force of gale wind. "What the hell were you thinking?"

CHAPTER SEVENTEEN

Her blood boiling, it had taken everything Hannah had in her not to explode all over her *volunteer*. The last thing she needed to do was upset the horses. As it was she was pretty damn sure that Patience could sense her anger even though she'd tried to hide it. Most horses were incredibly sensitive animals which is what made them such great therapy aids. Some were even too sensitive. So much so that they would try to compensate for the student's shortfalls, which of course wasn't doing the student any good at all. Hannah hadn't wanted to upset Patience or any of the other horses in the stable with a temper tantrum.

But now, out here in the parking lot, all bets were off. She'd held her anger in for about as long as she could before spinning around and stabbing a finger at Dale's chest. "Who the hell do you think you are?"

A solid wall of muscle stood firm. "Someone who cares."

"That doesn't give you the right to use do-it-yourself psychoanalysis on my students. You could have pushed that kid completely over the edge. Could've sent him to places none of us could pull him back from. Could've made his situation a whole hell of a lot worse. And it all would've been sitting in my hands."

"But I didn't." His eyes remained trained on her. "He did what you wanted him to do. He got up, he got inside, and he got on the horse. And unlike a lot of men I've known, he's going to get better."

"Great." She flung her arms in the air and took a step back, sucking in a calming breath. "All's well that ends well. That won't cut it, not in my stable, and sure as hell not with my patients." Her hands fisted at her side. There weren't enough words to express how furious she was. "You have the unmitigated gall to ride in here off the street on your metallic steed and your do-gooder's sense of honor, and think you have all the answers. I'm the one with the training in psychology. I'm the one who does this for a living. I'm the one who was raised around horses, and I was scared shitless I could screw this up."

"You don't think I was scared?" Dale shortened the distance between them. His voice rougher, deeper. "I don't have a psych degree, I don't have a therapy license, but I know people. If you don't have someone's respect then you won't get anything done. You think your blood is boiling now? It's exactly how I felt watching that kid disregard you, ignore you, disrespect you. You could've stood here from now till next Thursday and you wouldn't have talked him into going inside. The kid's got an anger chip on his shoulder as big as the state of Texas."

"He's not the first or last angry kid I'm going to deal with. These things do not get cured overnight, and especially not with a lot of yelling and browbeating. It takes time, it takes patience, and it takes understanding for things to happen."

"That's right. And sometimes those things that happen are bad things. The entire world is not your Pollyanna Farraday country. Damn it Hannah, I couldn't do a damn thing to save Peter from himself, but I can sure as hell do something to help this kid!"

"What?" Now he was talking nonsense.

Sucking in a deep breath, he took a half step back, ran his hand across the back of his neck, and stepped up close to her again. "Not everything is won over with friendly loves and hugs and pats on the back. Sometimes you have to fight for what you want. And fight hard. Sometimes, it gets down dirty and nasty. The kid has been blanketed with love and kindness and people tiptoeing around the problem long enough. It was time for some tough love."

"And here we are again. Who the hell are you to make that kind of a judgment call?"

"A man who spent eight years in the United States Marine Corps. A man who understands what Semper Fi means. A man who understands the meaning of no man left behind. It's not just in physical battle. That kid's eyes are filled with hunger to be one of us. And today I gave that to him. For the first time in a long time, he had a choice to act like a warrior or wallow at being a victim."

"He's just a kid. What would you have done if he had not stood up? How would you have handled a more broken child?"

Dale leaned forward, their faces only inches apart. "I would have counted on you."

The shift from macho man know-it-all to expecting her to have his back threw her momentarily off stride. "So you go in willy-nilly breathing fire, and expect me to come in behind you and clean up the debris?"

"I see it more as hard meets soft. I have the roar of a lion and you have a heart of gold."

"That's it? That's your defense?" Once again she jabbed his chest with her finger. "I have news for you. Bark loud now and think it through later is not going to work for me."

Dale closed the last sliver of gap between them. "I don't know about that."

She sucked in a startled breath at his nearness, then held onto it as his mouth came crashing down on hers. Strong hands pulled her tightly against him, leaving no choice but to wrap her arms around him for balance.

Except the last thing she felt was balance. Stars danced before her eyes and she could swear she heard music in the background. Soft sweet music. Knowing she should pull back, step away, break the contact, didn't matter. Her lips tingled, her fingertips were eager to roam, and her toes curled in her boots. Wow. If this is what kissing was all about, then she'd never been kissed before.

• • • •

Somewhere in the back of Dale's mind, a still small voice desperately tried to make him stop. He needed to back up, back away, back off, and yet, right now he wasn't sure he cared.

Everything about Hannah in his arms felt right. Her mouth under his was the perfect mix of sweet and soft and hard and hungry. All the more reason why he had to stop, like it or not.

Letting his hands fall to his side, he managed a small step back. Still close enough to feel the heat between them, he sucked in a breath and retreated another step. He needed some distance. Thinking was not an option at the moment. At least not with the head on his shoulders. "I'm sorry." The words tumbled easily.

Eyes closed even after he'd put some distance between them, Hannah slowly lifted her chin. Leveling her gaze with his, he was delighted to see the same yearning inside him reflected in her eyes.

"Car won't start?" Catherine came out of the building. "Do you need me to give you a lift home?"

Hannah sprang backward. She had that same frightened look as a deer caught in bright lights. "Uh, no."

Scanning the car and then Hannah, Catherine's brows knit together in confusion. "Did you forget something?"

"No," Dale answered. "We were just discussing Clark."

Still frowning, Catherine looked from Dale back to Hannah.

"How to handle his sessions," Hannah said.

Catherine nodded slowly, then shrugged. "Well, if you don't need my help, I'll get back to work."

"Thanks," Hannah and Dale echoed. The two remained standing in place until Catherine had disappeared.

Hannah didn't know what to say. She hadn't expected the kiss, and she certainly hadn't expected to respond the way she had. This was a guy she'd only known a few days, and she melted into his arms like butter in a frying pan. "We better get back to the ranch."

Dale merely nodded, then scurried around her to open the driver door.

"Thanks." What she really wanted to do was toss him the car keys and walk back to the ranch. Fresh air would go a long way to clear her thoughts. Sitting in an enclosed space only a couple of feet away from the man who had just kissed her socks off wasn't going to do much to help sort out the rush of emotions surging inside her.

Keeping her eyes on the road, she was thankful that at least the short distance made for a quick drive home. Pulling in front of the house, she turned the engine off and quickly hopped out of the car.

"Listen," Dale grabbed hold of her hand before she could step onto the porch, "I need to say something before we go inside and extend this awkward silence for the rest the night."

Hannah nodded. She briefly considered insisting there was nothing to be awkward about, but that would've been an outright lie and they both knew it.

"I'm sorry." Dale hung onto her hand. "About a lot of things. I'm sorry I overstepped my bounds, even though I believe I was right. I should have spoken to you first, told you what I was thinking. Let you decide how you wanted to handle it."

She hadn't expected that. His words did as much to warm her heart as his hand did to warm her blood. "Thank you."

"And about that kiss."

The mere mention of it had her lips tingling again.

"I should apologize for that." He shook his head. "Wait, let me rephrase. I'm not sorry that I kissed you. I'm only sorry about the timing. Besides the fact that you deserve to be kissed in the sunshine, or under the stars, with roses and music, and not in the heat of battle, there are a lot of things going on in my life right now that I'm not at liberty to share. That, more than anything, is why I had no right to kiss you."

If his words were meant to brush aside what had just happened, they'd done the complete opposite. Right now she wanted little more than to kiss him again. Wasn't that just asking for trouble?

CHAPTER EIGHTEEN

Reluctantly, Dale let go of Hannah's hand. He didn't even have the right to do that. Hell, after only knowing Hannah a few days he barely had the right to talk to her. And considering the mess he was in, waiting for somebody else to come up with the evidence to keep him from a life in witness protection after testifying, was enough reason to not even become casual friends. Even if that much was already too late.

They were halfway through dinner before Dale realized that having DJ show up for supper every night was not the norm. And according to Aunt Eileen, showing up early for supper was very unusual. He couldn't blame the guy for wanting to keep an eye on the situation himself. It was, after all, the people he loved most in the world who were at risk having Dale in their home.

Sean Farraday swallowed his last bite of pie. "What time is Brooks coming by tonight?"

"He's not." Aunt Eileen stood from the table, picking up her plate. "Nora is coming for today's bloodwork. She should be here soon."

"Today's only the third day," Dale picked up his empty plate, "and I'm already feeling like a pin cushion."

"I'm sure you are, but it's the only way to tell when you're well enough to leave."

Dale flashed the family matriarch a teasing grin. "Trying to get rid of me already?"

Flustered, Aunt Eileen's eyes widened and her jaw went slack until she realized he was teasing her. Rolling her eyes, she whacked him lightly across the elbow. "As far as I'm concerned, you're welcome to stay as long as you'd like. But if riding out on that contraption all the way to China is what you want to do, then being pricked every day is the only way to do it."

Carrying his dish to the sink, DJ looked to Dale. "What did Brooks have to say about yesterday's blood test results?"

"Not much really." Without thinking, Dale turned on the water and began rinsing off dishes. "We're waiting for my Warfarin levels to be high enough that I no longer need the Heparin injections. As of yesterday's blood test, we're not there yet. But he gave no indication of how much longer it might be."

Hannah opened the dishwasher door to load the rinsed dishes.

A plate in either hand, Aunt Eileen turned and smiled. "Isn't this a lovely sight. Busy people cleaning up the dinner dishes, and I'm not one of them."

Looking up from the dishwasher, Hannah waived an arm at her aunt. "You go watch something on TV or play cards with Uncle Sean. The rest of us can handle the kitchen tonight."

For a short second her aunt looked as though she was going to object, but she merely handed the dishes off to Hannah and marched slowly to the den.

While DJ brought more dishes over from the table, Finn put the leftovers in glass containers to stack in the fridge, Dale filled the empty pots with warm soapy water to soak, and Hannah reached for the old radio that had sat on the kitchen shelf for as long as she could remember. Immediately one of her favorite country songs came on, and she sang along softly, almost mumbling the lyrics.

"You have a pretty voice." Dale turned off the faucet to better hear her.

DJ placed the last empty dishes into the sink. By the time he'd returned to the table with a sponge he was humming along with Hannah. "That's a catchy tune. What's the name?"

"Not sure." Hannah shrugged. "I like the chorus where it goes *If you were mine I'd always be there*."

"Sort of gets in your head and won't let go." DJ paused, listening.

Finn put the last food container into the fridge, and standing beside his brother, focused on the song. "Definitely one of those songs I can see myself humming for the next few weeks. Who sings it?"

"Some new group." Hannah stuffed the dish rag over one of the cabinet handles. "Their name is Tow the Line."

Finn and DJ froze in place. Only the startled look in their eyes implied something was not right. Immediately, DJ whipped out his phone and began tapping away.

"Is something wrong?" Hannah asked.

DJ swiped the phone once and again, and then letting out a heavy sigh lifted the phone face out for Finn to see. "It's her. Do you think Ethan knows?"

"Ethan?" Hannah inched around her cousins to look at the face of the phone. Nothing struck her at first glance. Certainly nothing that her cousin finishing out his time in the Marines in California would need to know. "I don't get it. What am I looking at?"

"I had to dig a little, but one of the backup singers is Fancy Langdon."

"And?"

"She's Brittany's mother."

Hannah had to think a minute. Why did this matter? "Is this a big deal?"

Finn shrugged and looked at his brother. "What do you think?"

"I honestly don't know." DJ looked at the screen again. "But I think we'd better talk to Ethan."

Dale stepped up next to DJ as well. "Anything I can help with?"

"Nothing you can do that I couldn't do."

Hannah looked from Dale to DJ, thinking what an odd come back. "Is there something you two aren't telling me?"

DJ pinched his brow. "When is Grace coming home?"

"Saturday morning. Why?"

"No reason. Just curious." DJ ran his hands along the back of his neck.

Not that Hannah believed DJ's answer for a minute, but she was even less inclined to believe him when he shifted gears by calling Brooks for an update and stepped outside.

Hannah looked to Finn. "Is he upset about Fancy or Grace?"

Her cousin shook his head and even though he wasn't asked, Dale smiled and shrugged.

An odd reaction for someone who shouldn't know anything. Or did he?

● ● ● ●

With the kitchen cleaned up and DJ on the porch still, Dale decided a little fresh air was in order. "I think I'll go outside and stretch my legs."

Finn nodded, but eyes squinting, Hannah looked suspiciously through the window at DJ and back to him before nodding as well.

"I see. Uh huh. All right." DJ pinched his brow again. "We'll have to play this by ear. Thank you, bro."

"Not good news?"

"That all depends. Brooks is pleased with your progress in general."

"I detect a *but* coming."

DJ nodded. "He's projecting you'll need a few extra days here."

Dale dropped into the nearest rocker. "I'm sure I can get the shots somewhere else."

"Too risky." DJ shook his head.

"Not really. Nobody knows I threw a clot and am on Heparin."

DJ blew out a sigh. "Have you heard anything more from the DA?"

"Nothing you want to hear."

"Well," DJ looked his friend in the eye and sighed, "if nothing's changed, all we can do is wait and see how long we can keep this thing quiet."

A part of him knew DJ was right. Odds were pretty slim anyone was looking for him, and even if they were, a cattle ranch wouldn't be the first place to look regardless if his old partner was the chief of police. But another part wanted to get as far away as possible from these nice people to avoid any chance of bringing harm down on them. Especially one. "You sure?"

"I'm not sure of a blessed thing, but it's what we're going to do for now." DJ turned to open the screen door. "Coming?"

"No. It's been a long day. I think I'll just sit here for a short while."

With a nod, DJ stepped inside and the screen door slammed shut behind him.

One thing that Dale loved about the West Texas sunset and being this far away from a big city was the splattering of bright stars in the sky. Staring off in the distance, watching the sun kiss the horizon and waiting for darkness to fall, he felt a rushing pressure against his leg.

Another clot was the first thing to cross his mind, but before he had time to process the options, he felt the nudge and tap at his knee and looked down. "Well, how are you today?"

A soft grumble that wasn't quite a whine and wasn't quite a bark came from the furry pup.

"You're a talker, are you?" He scratched under the puppy's chin. "Guess you may have a bit of husky in you too."

The puppy circled his leg and then nudged Dale's hand with his nose.

"Wonder where Mama is?" Continuing to scratch the puppy behind his ears, he scanned the area for the mother. "Guess you're on your own tonight." He was going to have to remember to ask the family what this fellow's name was, and if there were more to the litter.

The fuzzy guy curled up beside Dale's foot, resting his chin across his boots and thoroughly enjoying the scratch. "I bet you will give me all of two or three hours to stop doing this, won't you?" Dale wasn't completely sure, but he thought the dog opened one eye and looked up at him before flopping back down again.

Enjoying the relaxed moment with the puppy nearly as much as the little dog clearly was, Dale was startled by the sound of his cell phone. Usually he was the one to check in with the DA and no one else had the number. The unexpected call had him on alert. Not that he expected his enemies to have found him here at the ranch, but just the same he stood and walked to the edge of the porch, scanning the distance left to right and across the other way as he answered the phone. "Yes?"

"Thought you might like to know," the DA said easily, "the henchmen who witnessed Joe pull the trigger is in ICU."

"Apparently he was expendable."

"A loose end perhaps. Either way, we've got double guards on duty. If he wakes up and we dangle the WITSEC carrot, we might flip him."

Disappearing into witness protection would most likely be the only way for that guy to stay alive if the mob wanted him dead. "What are his chances of waking up?"

"50-50. If you believe in prayer, start praying."

That was something he had a lot of practice at. "Thanks for the update."

"Dale?" Her voice lowered slightly. "I won't let you down."

"Back at you." Disconnecting the call, he slipped the phone into his breast pocket. Hopefully this time, luck and a prayer would be enough.

CHAPTER NINETEEN

Unless she was dealing with a student, waiting patiently was not one of Hannah's strengths. She'd waited in the den with the rest of the family for nearly half an hour for Dale to come back inside and finally gave up with any pretense of watching whatever show was on television. With some lame excuse about heading for the barn, she made her way outside.

At first glance she didn't see Dale on the porch or on the path and wondered if he was in the barn. Then she spotted movement to the right of the path. Hands in his pockets, his back to her, Dale stared off in the distance.

Having grown up with two older brothers, she understood the concept of man cave. Usually when one of her brothers was upset, or one of her cousins, they'd withdraw into something they love to do on their own. For all she knew this was one of those times for Dale. But something deep inside wouldn't allow her to turn around and go back into the house alone. Instead, she carefully went down the steps and across the path. She'd only made it halfway when he turned around to face her.

"I was hoping that was you."

Six little words and she had to bite back the urge to grin like a fool. "Wasn't sure if I should interrupt."

"Watching the sunset and the stars. Something that's always better with company." He flashed a sweet smile that almost made her knees wobble. "Everything is so peaceful here."

"You mean nothing like life in the city?" The man was so tight lipped about his recent life, all this secretiveness was starting to unnerve her.

"Something like that." He turned his attention forward once again. "What do you dream of?"

Once again, he'd deflected her inquiries. Why did she bother trying? On a silent sigh, she gave in to his line of questioning. "You mean when I sleep, or when I think about winning the lottery

The comment drew a chuckle from him and a glance in her direction. "Okay, one dream—win the lottery. When you think of the rest of your life, what do you picture?"

"That's a tough question." She had to pause a moment. "I guess I always thought in short term goals. Finish school, finish my hours, get my license, find steady work." This time she looked off into the distance a second before turning back to face him. "Long term—to make a difference. To help my students have a better life. Help those people who have fallen through the cracks."

"The Clarks of this world?" he asked.

"Yes and no. Don't get me wrong, I want very badly to help Clark. But there are some people out there who don't have mothers and fathers with good insurance or solid bank accounts. There are men and women, and sadly children, who have been hurt and broken and maybe even abandoned. If not physically then emotionally. And there are some who are drowning in their own despair. It's those people who need folks like my cousin Connor, his wife, Grace, me, and anybody else who will stand with them."

Smiling at her, Dale tipped his head slightly as though that would make him see her more clearly. "You really are amazing. I thought that the first time I watched you work with the horses, the way you are with your family, and today with your students. You're quite the woman."

Her family always told her things like that. Of course any guy in college anxious to get into her pants had showered her with flattery, but these complements came with no strings other than friendship. "There's nothing special about me."

"You are so very wrong about that. You are beautiful inside and out."

Heat rose to her cheeks. She needed to redirect the conversation. "What about you? What are your dreams?"

"Until recently I didn't think I had dreams anymore."

She waited briefly for him to say something else but decided he needed a little prompting. "Something has changed?"

"Maybe." He shifted around to face her fully. "Looks like I'm going to be staying on longer than we thought."

A flash of exhilaration at a chance to spend more time together fizzled out at the thought of why. "Is something wrong?"

"No. I just need more time for the medicine to kick in so I won't need the shots anymore."

Was it terribly wrong for her to be happy the medicine was taking too long to work? "Will you be staying here or going back to the B&B?"

"Here." He reached down and took hold of her hand. "Do you mind?"

She shook her head. She liked being this near, and the feel of her hand in his. Probably more than she should.

"You know enough about me to know my life right now is… complicated. There are things I'd like to share, but I can't. Still, I want you to know—you—this place," he waved his arm towards the house, "and this family are very special. I'll treasure you all always."

A sick feeling twisted in the pit of her stomach. "That sounds terribly ominous." Whatever the hell he was hiding and whatever connection it was that he and DJ had, her gut told her none of it was good.

● ● ● ●

"Looks to me like those two are getting awfully friendly." Eileen rinsed her glass and set it in the dishwasher. She'd been watching Hannah and Dale carefully all evening. Something had shifted today. She couldn't put her finger on it. At one point she thought there was more distance between them and the next thing there appeared to be more familiarity. Neither made sense.

"This was so much easier when the dog was around," she muttered to herself.

Sean came to stand beside her and lifted the lid on the pie plate. "I wouldn't worry about them. Hannah's got a good head on her shoulders. She knows he's not going to be sticking around long."

Except it wasn't Hannah's head that Eileen was worried about. "Do you know what exactly is going on between DJ and Dale?"

Sean's jaw tensed. After all these years, she easily recognized when he was torn inside.

"You've made a promise," she said softly.

"I have." The way he studied her, she knew he was thinking about breaking that promise.

"DJ told you why he's hiding out here?"

Sean hesitated, but nodded.

"It's serious? Strike that. Stupid question. Is it dangerous?"

Her brother-in-law pressed his lips tightly then blew out a sigh. "Not now, but it could be. The less details we know, the better for everyone, especially Dale. That's the only reason I would agree not to share with you or the children."

For Sean Farraday to keep a secret from his entire family, that secret had to be something big. She glanced out the window at the two people walking back to the house. Lord how she hoped whatever everybody was hiding wasn't something that would break Hannah's heart.

● ● ● ●

"It's all settled." Catherine caught up with Dale and Hannah near the back porch. "I've been working on it almost nonstop since Clark agreed to participate."

"The games?" Hannah asked.

Holding up a folder, Catherine grinned like the Cheshire cat. "Everything. We're registered for the events in Houston. I've blocked out a long weekend in three weeks for our local event."

"You've been busy."

Stepping onto the porch, Catherine pulled a few pages from the file. "I've worked on flyers, sign-up sheets, marketing plans." She shoved the pages back in the folder. "It just came together so easily. I talked to Grace over the phone and she's already rolling with it. Your cousin is amazing. She's rattling off newspapers, TV interviews, you name it. We are going to get great publicity."

Dale held the back door open for everyone.

"And," Catherine continued without skipping a beat, "I've already done handwritten invitations to the donor list you gave me."

"Donor list?" Hannah must've missed something.

"Yes. It was Grace's idea. We're going to turn the games into a fundraising luncheon. A big barbecue with prizes and lots of fun. What better way to give people everywhere a chance to see what we can do up close and personal."

Hannah stared at the flyers that Catherine spread across the table. One by one the rest of the Farradays circled around the table, passing the flyers around, oohing and aahing. Within a few minutes all were gabbing excitedly. They were really going to pull this off.

Catherine looked to Dale. "I do hope you'll be able to stay with us?"

His face washed with surprise. "Well, I can certainly help the rest of this week."

"If we're going to have more students involved besides Melody and Clark, we're going to need a few volunteers." Catherine looked to Aunt Eileen. "And I was thinking the Ladies Afternoon Social Club might be a good place to start."

Aunt Eileen rubbed her hands together. "Oh, I think that will be so much fun. And I bet the sisters would have fun helping too. They might have to take turns, but I bet they'd love it."

From the corner of her eye, Hannah caught DJ staring pointedly at Dale. All their hard work hiding Dale at the ranch would be shot to hell if half the town volunteered. Wasn't this a fun little predicament?

CHAPTER TWENTY

"**I**s it my turn to shuffle?" Ruth Ann looked left then right. "Who just dealt?"

"I did." Meg tossed her cards to Dorothy. "Aunt Eileen deals and Dorothy shuffles. You're next."

"Got it."

"Woman," Dorothy chuckled, "you'd think you hadn't played cards in a year instead of a week."

"Hey," Ruth Ann shrugged, "with every new gray hair I lose a few brain cells. Besides, it's been ages since we've gone from Saturday to Saturday without a weekday card game. Doesn't take long to get out of practice."

"Ha," Eileen barked, "that'll be the day."

This time when Ruth Ann shrugged, there was an impish twinkle in her eye. The woman never could bluff.

"Whoa," Nora whistled softly. "Did someone win the lottery in town and not tell us?"

All heads turned to watch the white Lincoln Continental park. By the time the woman appeared from the backseat, every eye in the place was on her.

"As if the car hadn't been a giveaway, but that woman is most definitely not from any place close to around here." Sally May tracked the woman's every move.

"Jeez," Nora whispered, "that's a Prada handbag."

"Probably real," Meg volunteered.

Eileen looked at the contemporary black purse. "You sure?"

"It's impossible to tell without looking inside, but my guess is anyone who can afford either side of 75k for a car and rides in the backseat, doesn't need to be buying knock offs from Ebay."

The woman in question came to her feet, removed a jacket,

and handed it to the driver. A few words were exchanged and then she glided over the walkway to the front door.

"Definitely a real handbag," Meg agreed.

Sally May squinted at the woman's back as she walked away. "How can you tell from here?"

"Because she's wearing a St. John's suit."

Ruth Ann set her cards down and crossed her arms. "Someone want to tell me in plain English what all this talk means?"

"It means," Sally May turned to her friend, "that woman's outfit costs more than a prize bull."

Ruth Ann let out a whistle an octave louder than Nora had.

"Wonder what the heck she's doing here?" Eileen couldn't imagine this lady was a tourist interested in visiting local ghost towns.

"Do you think it has anything to do with Joanna's book?" Dorothy asked.

Eileen shook her head. "She's in Dallas finalizing the wedding of the century. Surely anyone she works with would know that."

"Besides," Meg chimed in, "from what Joanna says, her editor sounds like a nice average woman about our age. This lady looks like she's the winner of a Jackie Onassis lookalike contest."

The moment the bell over the restaurant door jingled, Eileen and the rest of the Ladies Afternoon Social Club scrambled to spread their cards, toss chips, and look like they hadn't been staring at the stranger. Eileen and Meg were the only two facing the door. When Meg kicked her, she peeked over the edge of her cards in time to see Abbie the café owner talking to the newcomer and pointing to the back. The only table in the back with people at it was theirs.

"She's coming this way," Nora mumbled through clenched teeth and a phony smile.

"Excuse me," the soft voice nothing like what Eileen expected said. "Which of you nice ladies would be Margaret Farraday?"

"That would be me." Meg stood.

"Oh good. I stopped at your establishment and the note said you could be found here."

"Yes. Are you looking for a room?"

The woman smiled as if there was a private joke between them. "You could say that. I have a reservation."

"Reservation?" Meg pushed away from the table and pulled out her phone. "I'm terribly sorry, I don't remember any..." She circled the table to stand beside her guest. "What is your name?"

"Marie Stewart."

Meg's head shot up. "Oh, dear. I have you down as coming in for the Capaill horse show and games in two weeks."

A deep frown drew the woman's brows together as she too pulled out her phone and began tapping away. "Excuse me a moment." Taking two steps from the table and turning her back, she spoke into her phone. "Audrey, what's on your calendar for today? ... Uh huh... I see... And in two weeks? Okay, you'd better call Herb and Nancy and tell them I won't be making it to dinner this evening. Send them a little something for my apologies."

Meg looked to her aunt, and Eileen realized immediately what her concerns were. If this lady was here for the equine games, she had to be one of the donors, and the stables were woefully unprepared for a show.

● ● ● ●

"Excellent, Melody. Very well." Hannah had to admit the girl's huge grins at the smallest accomplishment were enough to make anyone's day. "That's it for today."

Melody's mom stood on the other side of the arena gate, smiling proudly at her daughter. "She is doing so well with you."

"Thank you. That's nice to hear." Pushing the latch on the gate, Hannah held it open for Dale to lead Melody back to the mounting blocks. "She's so very excited about the horse show too."

"Yes, she is. I can't thank you enough for putting all this

together."

"My pleasure." And it truly was.

Melody came hurrying down the wooden ramp. "Patience is a good horse, Mama."

"Yes, she is."

"Miss Catherine has your snack for you at the tables inside." Hannah pointed to the lounge area by the offices. The other day at one of Melody's lessons, Catherine noticed Melody looking at the granola bar on Catherine's desk and now post-lesson treats were the norm for all students if they wanted. Melody wanted.

"I'll take care of Patience." Dale smiled down at her.

The last few days working together with the horses and the new students had been an incredible high for Hannah, but having Dale around was simply icing on the cake. The guy had a great sense of humor, and even though he seemed to need to keep secrets, especially about his recent past, she'd loved all his stories growing up with a military strict dad and a card-carrying hippy mom. Some were a little heart wrenching, but most were just plain funny, like the time when he was about three and got away from his mom, running up the aisle calling "Daddy" in the middle of a formal promotion ceremony.

"We've got time till Clark gets here." She scratched behind the horse's ear. "I'll help."

Her reward was another bright smile and a chirping phone. "Hello." Hannah put the call on speaker.

"We've got to move fast," Aunt Eileen said on the other end of the line.

Hannah stopped in her tracks. "What?"

"Listen. This lady, Marie Stewart, was on her way to the ranch—"

"What?" Hannah spun around and scanned the stables.

"I said listen. She got her dates confused. We figured from the way this lady is dressed she's got to be one of those donors y'all are courting."

That was an understatement. Hannah hurried to catch up with

Dale and Patience.

"So, I've put in some phone calls. Meg is buying us some time by taking Marie back to the B&B for mid-morning tea and scones."

Hannah set the phone on the rail and reached for a brush. "Scones?"

"Biscuits. Whatever!" Aunt Eileen's frustration rang loud and clear. "Will you stop interrupting?"

"Sorry." She rolled her eyes skyward, wishing her aunt would skip a chapter or two and get to the epilogue.

Dale stopped picking out the horse's hoof and straightening beside her, placed a sweet kiss on her cheek, then whispered, "Sorry. You're hard to resist when you make those cute faces."

Holding back a big grin, she brushed the horse's rump and tried to focus on her aunt's call.

"Are you there?" Aunt Eileen asked.

"Yes, sorry. You were saying."

"The ladies club is on their way to the stables. Frank is doing a few miracle briskets and Abbie will bring them over later with his mustard potato salad. Toni is packing up all the cake balls she has—the ones with booze—to hand out. People don't hold their checkbook closed so tightly when they've had a nip or two."

Ever since the incident with Toni's late husband, the idea of the boozed cake balls tended to rattle the Farraday brothers. Hannah hadn't made up her mind yet. But from the sounds of it, she was about to get her chance to decide for herself.

"I've put out the word we need to work fast. My next call is to Catherine. I don't know how many of your students we can get here on short notice—"

"For what?"

"I'm getting there." She could almost hear her aunt tapping her foot. "We're going to put on that horse show. Y'all are going to set up as best as possible. I've told Finn and Connor to bring the bleachers we use for the ranchathon. Folks are chipping in more food, and the sisters closed the store and are bringing out decorations."

"Aunt Eileen, slow down."

"There's no time!" Her aunt huffed loud enough to be heard in East Jerusalem. "We can do this. Have Dale help with the bleachers. Catherine will take care of the phone calls. The Brady boys and a couple of the Rankin kids and Stacey will fill in for bodies where we're short participants."

If any other person in the world had told her this plan, Hannah would have given them a psychiatric evaluation, but from her aunt Eileen, Hannah's mind was already rolling forward. "I'll ask Melody to stay. I bet she'll love the chance, and Clark is coming in an hour or so. I bet he'll do it."

"See!" Aunt Eileen's enthusiasm was contagious. "We're going to wow this woman's socks off and then she'll be throwing money at us."

That or torpedo the entire business plan in an afternoon.

Dale slipped the pick into a nearby bucket and hovered beside Hannah. She was finding it harder and harder to think when he stood this close to her.

"That's it," Aunt Eileen said, her voice more calm. "You get chopping. Love you, little girl."

"Love you too." Hannah reached for the phone and placed it in her pocket.

"It sounds like we've got our work cut out for us." Dale didn't touch her and yet the fire in his eyes had her warming from the inside out.

She bobbed her head. "I'll finish up here. You'd better go help Uncle Sean and Finn. We've got a little less than an hour before you'll have to make yourself scarce."

Pressing his lips tightly together, Dale's thoughts were almost too easy to read. He didn't like having to hide out. She still didn't know what from, but she'd learned enough about him to know it had to be something considerably more serious than a few outstanding parking tickets.

"It's okay. Go," she said.

Dale hesitated a moment before nodding and trotting out the main door.

What Hannah didn't know was how easy would it be to say *go* when she knew he wouldn't be coming back?

CHAPTER TWENTY-ONE

The whole idea was insane and yet damned if the Farradays didn't seem to be pulling it off. The portable bleachers were loaded on a flatbed in no time at all.

"How's the leg?" Finn asked.

Dale actually glanced down. He'd forgotten all about it. As a matter of fact, after a week on the ranch, he'd forgotten that not so very long ago he was in a hospital bed in the ICU fighting for his life. "Right as rain."

Both Connor and Finn flashed a thumbs up.

"Let's get moving with this. We can use the extra manpower unloading but people should be crawling around here like ants pretty soon."

Sooner than any of them had thought. The truck pulled up to the rear side of the arena and there already had to be ten or fifteen women inside scurrying around like, well, a colony of ants. The good thing was that everyone seemed so focused on their jobs that no one noticed an extra man in jeans and boots. Of course, the hat probably helped shield his face.

Keeping his head down, they managed to unload the truck in a fraction of the time it had taken to load.

"Yoo hoo." A short and stout blonde with a hairdo as high as it was wide and a grin the size of her face, waving and calling at them, ran across the arena as quickly as her little legs could carry her.

Dale figured he'd draw more attention to himself if he ran for the hills, so instead he spun about, grabbed hold of the tool box and crouching, tightened the lugs and bolts on the first set of bleachers.

"We've got some banners and we need a couple of you strong

handsome type to climb up on the ladder." The woman sucked in a few deep breaths between words.

"Of course, Sister." Sean gestured to his sons. "Why don't you two help Sister and we'll finish off over here."

"Yes, sir."

"Sister," another female voice called out.

"Yes, Sissy?"

Sissy? Dale had to turn and take a peek.

A tall slender redhead, cupping her hands around her mouth, yelled from halfway across the arena. "Ask them if they have a stapler. I forgot ours."

"Okie dokie, Sissy."

Tools in hand, Dale buried his head under the bleachers. Sister and Sissy. He wasn't at all sure if he wanted to know more about that or not. For the next hour he ducked out of doors, took the long route around buildings to help gather supplies, and did his best to remain helpful but unseen. When DJ's pregnant sister-in-law put her fingers to her lips and blew a whistle that could have alerted the Dallas PD and announced. "incoming fifteen minutes," Dale knew it was time to make himself seriously scarce. "I'll be in the stables now if anyone needs me."

"Thanks, man." Finn slapped him on the shoulder. "One of us will be in to help shortly."

"No problem. I can start pulling the saddles and other tack."

"Sounds like a plan."

Dale paused a moment to look around at the arena. The place looked like a poster for Americana gone wild. It looked fantastic. "Amazing," he muttered.

"Yeah," Finn smiled and nodded. "You should see the town in a real crisis."

"I can only imagine."

"They're here," sounded from in the distance and bodies started running every which way. A couple of teens came walking past him leading horses already saddled and ready to ride. Turning the other way Dale spotted the trailer in the back. He'd been so engrossed in watching the town come together, he never noticed the horse trailers pulling up and the teens working as hard as the adults to help out.

It wasn't just the Farradays who were material for a mid-century sitcom. The whole bloody town could have been characters in one of those barnyard musical movies. What Dale didn't get was, if this was how DJ grew up, why the heck had the man bothered at all with a major metropolitan police force. Any fool could see he belonged here.

A few more car doors slammed and Dale took another second to look up. White Lincoln. That had to be the money bags that had everyone throwing this little charity shindig together at the last minute. He couldn't see the woman's face, but he recognized money fifty yards out and this woman reeked of it.

Bypassing the incoming crowd, Dale slipped out the side door to go the long way into the stables. "Let the show begin."

• • • •

"Marie." Mrs. Hampton threw her arms around her friend. "So good to see you."

Chuckling, the potential donor hugged her friend then stepped back, shaking her head. "I can't believe I got the dates crisscrossed."

"Well, at least you're going to see Clark in action and some of the work these folks can do."

"Yes," Marie Stewart nodded. "I know Hannah here is great." The woman glanced around the arena then up at the rafters and cocking her head, back toward the pastures. "And it looks like she found a place worthy of her talents."

Linked elbow to elbow, the two women marched off chatting and laughing to the VIP seating area.

"She's really very nice." Meg leaned in closer.

"Oh, yeah. You should see her with children. She must sit on the board of every children's and woman's charity in North Texas.

She's always chairing some committee or other, or hosting a gala or auction. I see her name in the papers all the time. Great lady." Hannah had been a little nervous the very first time she'd met Mrs. Stewart. Her reputation proceeded her and with Hannah being 100% country girl and this lady obviously big city society, she had been more than nervous. But from the first *how do you*, Mrs. Stewart had made her feel totally at ease.

"We'd better get this show on the road. Grace Farraday, former multiyear junior barrel racing champion, and Finn Farraday, local rodeo champion will be the guest judges."

Each of Hannah's students, as well as her niece Stacey, one of the Rankins, and a couple of the Bradys, went through the paces of an equitation class. In the arena, more than one rider at a time showed how well they handled the horses and how well they transitioned from walk to trot and reverse direction. Each beamed with their ribbons won.

To show the skills of the Capaill horses, Connor and a couple of the neighboring ranchers put on a little cutting show for Mrs. Stewart. But the piece de resistance was the final event with Clark. More than adaptive riding, the kid was showing what he could do. Truth was, more than Hannah had expected. She thought he'd been holding back on her. Now she was sure. On an English saddle, he did a jumping demonstration, trotting over low cross rails. Without the use of stirrups to support his feet, to jump like that required both excellent balance and strong inner thigh muscles to lift a rider off the horse's back. Clark nailed it. The sight was especially impressive, and when he was done, the entire audience, including Marie Stewart, were on their feet.

"Fantastic." Marie Stewart clapped madly. "Can we go see him?"

"Sure we can," Clark's mother answered quickly, then turned to Hannah. "Right?"

"Absolutely." At this point, if the woman had asked permission to streak through the arena, Hannah would have given it.

"Come on." Adele Hampton led the way off the bleachers, then across the arena, chatting nonstop the whole way.

"There you are." Marie Stewart came to stop beside her friend's son. "You did a fabulous job. I couldn't be more proud of you if you were my son."

"Thanks, Mrs. H." Clark didn't say much, but Hannah could see the satisfaction in his eyes, the look that only comes from conquering and mastering your fears.

"A job well done should always be rewarded." Pulling her hand from her pocket, Marie Stewart flipped a silver coin at the young man. "Dobro, Clark. Dobro."

● ● ● ●

"Wow. A 1935 silver dollar." Clark's voice carried across the walkway for Dale to hear.

Whirling in place, Dale searched the crowded stall across the way for the giver of the coin. The only face he did not recognize was the middle-aged brunette in an expensive red suit that he'd seen climbing out of the Lincoln. The next words out of her mouth had been etched in Dale's memory. When the lady in red uttered the foreign phrasing, her voice dropped low. So low that even now, this close with no doors between them, if he were not looking at her, it would be hard for him to determine if it were a man or woman speaking, but he had no doubts. This was the same voice.

Holy crap. He'd found the head of one of North Texas' most dangerous crime organizations in the middle of blinking nowhere. He had to think fast. This time his phone recorder wasn't turned on, and there was no way anyone would believe that Marie Stewart, darling of the children's charity circuit, was the head of the Famiglia crime organization.

Hell, he still wasn't sure he believed it. Running his options quickly around in his head, the best thing would be for Hannah to record the woman talking. Today's sophisticated voice recognition would most likely be able to match it to the recording he had made of the shooting.

Turning to face the teen in the stall with him, Dale lowered his voice. He needed to get a hold of DJ and the DA without drawing any attention to himself. "I need to run. Do you have this, or do I need to get one of the others to come help?"

The kid looked at him as though Dale had asked if men wore cowboy boots in Texas before nodding. "Yeah, I got this."

Pulling out his phone, Dale tapped speed dial and stepped out of the stall, taking one last look at the women still gleefully chatting across the way. Just as he turned to race out of the building, Marie Stewart's gaze met his.

Shit.

CHAPTER TWENTY-TWO

The party had moved from inside the arena to the field behind Connor's house. The social club with the help of Frank and Abbie had enough tables set up to feed most of West Texas. The sisters had provided the red checkered tablecloths, napkins, paper plates, and plastic cutlery for all the guests.

"And you put all this together in a couple of hours?" Marie Stewart stood plate in hand, deliberating over her choices.

"It was a group effort," Hannah freely admitted. "You know what they say, it takes a village."

Marie laughed. "Don't I know it." The woman scooped a little of the potato salad, a bit of the brisket, a little of this, a little of that, all the while her eyes scanning the people at the surrounding tables and the straggling adults and children coming and going from the stables.

Standing behind the dessert table, Abbie set down a large foil tray and peeling the cover off, smiled at the guest of honor. "Life is short, ladies. Eat dessert first."

"I like that idea." Mrs. Hampton went straight for the blueberry cobbler. "These all look wonderful but I'm partial to blueberry."

"Then you're in luck. Frank, my cook, baked it this morning for the dinner rush."

"Oh you're definitely going to want to try that." Hannah picked a plate for herself and loaded it high. "Frank's cobbler is to die for."

"We only live once." Marie Stewart picked up a second plate and held it out for Abbie to fill. "Got any whipped cream back there?"

"You better believe it."

Still casually glancing about as Abbie scooped out the homemade whipped cream, Marie turned to Hannah. "So who was the gentleman working the stalls behind Clark's horse this afternoon?"

"I'm sorry," Hannah stabbed at the cobbler, "I didn't notice. We have quite a few locals helping out today."

"I see."

"I wonder if you mean the volunteer. What's his name?" Mrs. Hampton said. "David. I saw him helping in the stalls."

"David?" Marie repeated. "Has he volunteered here long?"

"A little while." Hannah answered honestly. A *while* being up for interpretation. "He's great with the kids."

"I'll second that." Mrs. Hampton waved a fork in the air. "He was great with Clark. If not for David, Clark would still be sitting in the front seat of the car giving me grief."

"You have such an excellent facility. Obviously the support staff as well." Mrs. Stewart took a bite of dessert. "Oh my. You weren't kidding. This is the best cobbler I've ever had."

"On behalf of Frank," Abbie said, "I thank you."

"Make sure to tell Frank I said you're welcome. And I will be back someday, maybe in two weeks for the real competitions."

"We would love to see you again," Hannah said.

"Actually I wouldn't mind meeting this David in person. Is he still around?" Marie toyed with her cobbler.

Hannah wasn't quite sure what to make of any of this. Dale was a handsome man who would catch the eye of any breathing female. And she'd heard more than one story about rich women and their boy toys. Though she had a hard time picturing Dale as anybody's toy. "I'm afraid I haven't seen him all day. But I'll make sure to introduce you next time." *Liar liar pants on fire.*

"Actually," Mrs. Hampton interjected, "I think I saw him going into the main house over there."

"Well, no matter. Next time will be just fine." Marie Stewart smiled.

Hannah was a relatively trusting person, but something in Mrs. Stewart's tone of voice told her next time would be anything but fine.

• • • •

"Are you absolutely, positively sure?" DJ said on the other end of the phone line.

Dale had been prepared for this. "More than absolute and more than positive. I'm telling you, there was no mistaking that voice. And she used the exact same phrasing as the person who spoke to Joe. I'm as floored as you are by this, trust me. I can't move around outside and risk being spotted. She's already seen my face. Odds are it won't be long before she confirms I'm not really dead and David the volunteer is Dale Johnson, prime witness for the prosecution."

"All right. I'll corral Hannah and get her to record Mrs. Stewart's voice without her knowledge. Then I'll have my deputies on alert. If she doesn't know who you are, today will just be business as usual. But if she recognized you, I don't want to be caught with our pants down."

Dale snatched one of the cake balls from a large tray on the counter. "I'll keep my head low, you can count on that."

"I'd better go track down my cousin and her donor. Keep me posted on what the DA says."

"Will do." The DA was next on Dale's list of people to contact.

The back door inched open and Brooks' wife, Toni, entered the kitchen. "I swear I spend more time in the bathroom than any other room in any house."

"No problem." Dale smiled and waited until she'd stepped into the tiny bath off the edge of the kitchen. When she pulled the door closed behind her and latched the lock, he turned a few steps away and once again pounded out a familiar number.

"Nothing new to report," the DA said without preamble.

"Not what I'm calling about. I know who the head of the crime organization is."

"Who?"

"You won't need to answer that," a deep, now familiar voice, sounded from across the room. "Put the phone down and kick it my way." Marie Stewart stood impeccably dressed, except for the gun in her hand.

Dale's thoughts galloped to Toni in the bathroom. Not willing to chance stray bullets, he did as he was told, set the phone on the ground and kicked it across the kitchen.

"Talk about dumb luck." Marie stomped her thousand dollar heel hard onto the phone. "Of all the equine instructors, and all the horse stables in the state, you would choose to volunteer at the only one I have any reason to visit."

"I guess you're just lucky that way." And he could use some of that luck to maneuver them out of proximity to Toni and the bathroom.

She strolled slowly to the left, closing in on him—and the bathroom door.

"If you fire that gun in here, the entire town is going to come running."

Marie cast a sideways glance to the back door that he hadn't heard her come in through. Impromptu most likely wasn't her best skill set. "My limo is out front."

Or maybe it was. As much as he disliked the idea of turning his back to her, he wanted out and away from Toni.

"Ah ah," the woman tsked. "Slowly. I want to see your fa—"

"Oh my God!" Sounded from the tiny bathroom.

Before Marie could turn to where the scream came from, the door flew open, hitting her in the arm at the exact moment the roar of laughter burst through the back door, the knob banging against the wall in synchronized rhythm with a single bullet discharging from Marie's flailing arm and breezing over Dale's head into the wall behind him.

"My water broke," Toni screeched. "Someone call Brooks!"

Dale lunged forward, and regaining her footing, Marie spun the gun in his direction. "Not so fast, Buster."

"Baby!" A woman with long gray hair pulled back in a sloppy pony tail screamed. "Our first grandbaby!"

Another taller woman, oblivious to Marie standing only a couple of feet away wielding a gun, rushed to Toni's side. "Dear, you need to sit down." The woman glanced up toward the counter. "For Lord's sake Ruth Ann, put that tray down. The cake balls can wait."

"But Sally May, the guests are waiting. Eileen said it's very important."

A more petite woman with short curly brown hair ran passed the lady with the tray to Toni's other side. "Ruth Ann, if you've got to take the cake balls outside, for heaven's sake go get Brooks while you're out there."

"Hold it!" Marie spun about, pointing the gun at the pregnant woman. "Nobody move or I'll shoot."

"I couldn't have said it better myself."

Marie turned to her left. Staring her in the face was the dangerous end of one police issue handgun and three long barreled rifles. Courtesy of DJ, Aunt Eileen, Grace and Hannah.

Shaking her head, Aunt Eileen lifted her chin at the women huddled across the kitchen. "Don't just stand there Ruth Ann. Go get Brooks!"

CHAPTER TWENTY-THREE

"You people are crazy," Marie screamed at the army of women pointing rifles at her.

"Maybe," Aunt Eileen flashed a toothy grin, "but it never hurts to remember, ranchers keep loaded weapons handy, and we know how to use them."

"And you can put those away now." DJ pointed toward the gun cabinet up the hall then turned and yanked at Marie's arms, spinning her to face Dale. "Would you like the honors?"

Dale's severe expression mirrored DJ's. Nodding, he stepped forward, and grabbing hold of the woman's arm walked toward the door. "You have the right to remain silent. Anything you say can and will be used against you in a court of law..."

"Talk about things are never boring around here. An hour ago I was coming home from a business trip, got pulled into judging a horse show I've heard nothing about, only to find myself backing up my brother on a raid." Grace handed her rifle over to DJ and waved her arm at Dale. "And, Dale, what are you doing here?"

"You know him?" Hannah asked.

"Of course I do." Grace pointed at her brother. "He used to be DJ's partner. Remember? The one in the hospital after the car accident?"

Aunt Eileen slapped her hand on her forehead. "Of course. How did I not make the connection? Now everything makes sense."

Maybe some things made sense.

Officer Reed came in from the rear. Brooks flew across the room, coming to a screeching halt in front of his wife. "Are you all right?"

Toni patted his chest. "Not bad for having contractions off

and on most of the afternoon."

"Oh my Lord, that's right!" Ruth Ann screeched again, "Our first grandbaby!"

Suddenly all the questions about Dale and Marie forgotten, Sally May went left, Dorothy went right and Grace and Aunt Eileen collided on route to Toni. For Hannah, the next few minutes were more of a blur than when she'd had to hold a gun to a woman she'd thought to be one of the nicest ladies on earth.

"Well don't just stand there. Let's get her into town." DJ ushered the crowd out of the house.

Like ants at a picnic, the family dispersed in different directions and vehicles.

"We'll take care of everything here and meet you in town later," Sally May assured them.

"Coming with us?" Aunt Eileen called over her shoulder to Hannah.

"I'll catch up with you." Her attention was on Dale. The prisoner secured in the backseat, Dale took a step from the driver's door, gave it a pat, and watched Reed pull away.

She didn't move. Not till the police car had passed under the new wrought iron sign did Dale turn around and walk toward her.

He looked dog tired. Watching one car after the other pull out and speed up the driveway, he came to a stop in front of her. "How is Toni?"

"On her way to have a baby."

"But she's okay?"

Hannah nodded.

For a second he looked over her shoulder and then without a word, pulled her tightly into his arms. "I was scared silly that something was going to happen to Toni and the baby. But when you came in with that rifle and Marie spun around, I was terrified she would rather go down shooting then be arrested. There isn't a word for the abject fear that clutched at me thinking she might take you down with her." His grip on her tightened and she buried her face in his shoulder.

"It's probably very similar to the shock that ran through me when I realized Aunt Eileen had us following DJ into the house to play Rambo with your life."

Dale chuckled. "She would make a good Rambo. I'm a bit surprised DJ let her."

"You don't know Aunt Eileen. We saw what was going on through the window just as DJ approached the house. The plan had been to surround her before anyone got hurt, but then Toni went into labor and…"

"Yeah, but I don't ever want to see you take a chance like that again." He leaned back just enough to look her in the eyes. "Promise me?"

"Does this mean you're sticking around long enough to see whether or not I keep the promise?"

He pulled her tightly against him again. "I'm not sure how much you've figured out. But the long and short of it is, I have to go back to Dallas and testify against her right-hand man for murder, and against her for giving the order. After that, if all goes the way it should, Marie Stewart and most of her organization will be spending a good long time in jail, and I'll be free to come back wherever I please."

A succession of short high-pitched yaps sounded just before the full force of a four-legged bundle of fur plowed into the back of Hannah's legs.

"Well, who is this?" She bent over to pet the puppy.

Dale crouched down beside her "Isn't he yours?"

"Mine?"

"Yeah, he's been coming out in the evenings to visit with me at your place. I thought he was a litter of your dogs."

"We don't have a litter."

"He's usually here with his mother." Dale glanced around and pointed behind Hannah. "There."

Off in the distance, halfway to the street, not one but two wolf mixed dogs sat watching them. "Oh my gosh." Hannah pushed her feet. "Those are the dogs."

"The dogs?"

As if they could hear from that far, Hannah was pretty sure both animals dipped their heads. Nodded.

"Did you see that?" Hannah turned to face him, both hands palm flat on his chest.

"The nod? Yeah. I wonder if they have a nervous tick or something. One of them did that to me the first night I saw it."

She turned back to the street and the dogs. "Where'd they go?"

"They're right..." Dale's stopped and scanned left then right. "They're gone. What's that all about?"

"It's a long story. And we have to get to town and meet up with the others."

The puppy yapped again, tail wagging, and tongue lolling. When neither Dale nor Hannah moved, the little guy yapped again and jumped up against them.

Dale looked around one more time, then bent down to pick up the pup. "I'm not totally sure, but I think he's ours now."

The puppy yapped, nodded, licked Dale's face and then scurried out of his arms and almost knocked Hannah over, crawling into her arms and licking her face too.

"Ours, you say?" Hannah smiled, squinting as the puppy loved on her. "I think I like the sound of that."

EPILOGUE

"**I** Finnegan George Farraday, take you, Joanna Marie Gaines, to be my wife…"

This ceremony made four out of five Farraday weddings in less than a year. Ian Farraday hadn't been all that surprised when Adam got married, or even Brooks. But when the rest of his cousins, one after the other, were struck by the love bug, Ian had to admit if he hadn't seen the passionate look in everyone's eyes for himself, he never would have believed true love could strike a family almost all at once.

Of course, nothing had been as surprising for him as showing up at the ranch a few weeks ago to meet the newest Farraday, baby Helen, and discovering his kid sister was head over heels in love. With a cop, no less. At least the guy would soon be joining the Tuckers Bluff police force. Not that Ian had anything against the Dallas PD, but as a Texas Ranger he understood better than anyone the risks a person takes when he wears a badge and a gun to work every day. Especially knowing Dale's intentions toward Hannah, Ian was dang glad the man wouldn't be working a big city any more.

"You may now kiss the bride."

For a few seconds, Ian wasn't sure Finn would remember they were in public, and from the way the preacher cleared his throat—loudly—it seemed he wasn't so sure either.

"Ladies and gentlemen, may I present for the first time in public, Mr. and Mrs. Finnegan Farraday."

"Finn married." Ian shook his head and turned to his sister beside him just in time to see Dale lean in for a quick peck on the lips and a promise in his eyes of more to come. As one of her older brothers, Ian preferred to think that promise was reflective of the ring Dale intended to put on her finger as soon as the nasty business with the Famiglia crime boss was over with. Not that Hannah knew anything about the ring.

Last night in the hotel bar, Dale had corralled their father and declared his plans to settle down in Tuckers Bluff, and when the time was right, ask Hannah to marry him. The funny thing was he seemed to think he needed time to win her over to the idea of marrying him. If this guy didn't know Hannah's answer right now would be a resounding yes, then there was more truth in the old expression love is blind than Ian had thought. Hell, even he could see the stars in her eyes every time she glanced in Dale's direction. When most girls were going from teen crush to crush, Hannah was all about the horses. Not anymore. His little sister was definitely all grown up. And when the heck had that happened?

Row by row, the guests exited the pews, and like cattle following the leader, worked their way through the receiving line and out the door to wait along the church steps.

"What's this?" Ian looked down at the cone shaped container his sister handed him filled with…something.

"Lavender." She grinned.

"For what?"

Hannah rolled her eyes skyward. "To throw, silly."

"It's eco-friendly." Dale came to stand on the steps beside Hannah, one arm comfortably looping around her waist. "At least that's what they tell me."

"I thought bird seed was the thing now?" Ian never understood why they stopped throwing rice. There were plenty of scientific studies to show it did no harm to birds.

Hannah wound her arm around Dale's middle and leaned in. "Bird seed might not be too bad for the birds, but apparently if you get a guest with a good arm, the seeds can hurt. And a lot of brides complain that it gets caught in their dress and other …fun places."

Now Ian really didn't like the way Hannah looked up at Dale grinning. TMI for a big brother.

"Move over, cuz." Two cones in one hand, DJ and his wife

Becky came to join the group. "You ready for some real work?"

"Ha ha ha." While Finn and Joanna were on their honeymoon, Ian requested vacation time to help out at the ranch. "Says the man who sits behind a desk most of his day."

DJ lowered his voice, "Finn says they're missing another calf."

"Only one?"

"Sure looks that way." DJ shrugged.

Ian didn't get it. Most rustlers took as much cattle as they could fit in a trailer. If it weren't his cousin telling him only one was unaccounted for, he'd assume there was a break in the fence line and the rancher was too stupid to figure it out.

"Here they come," Hannah squealed, sliding her arm away from Dale and preparing to bombard the young couple with lavender.

Following the bride and groom making a mad dash to the horse and buggy waiting to whisk them to the reception, the crowd continued to cheer and shower the couple until the carriage pulled away.

Ian, on the other hand, kept his eyes on his sister holding hands with Dale. He was starting to get used the idea of her as one half of a couple.

"I'm not sure who's going to make it to the altar first." DJ looked to Hannah and Dale. "Those two or Grace."

"He has to ask first."

"Should be sooner than everyone thinks."

Ian drew his gaze away from his sister to face his cousin. "You know something the rest of us don't?"

"Between the deposition from the guy who wound up in the hospital, the recording on Dale's phone, his deposition to the grand jury, and multiple eyewitnesses to Marie Stewart threatening to shoot Dale, she and several key players are plea bargaining as we speak." DJ crossed his arms.

"Don't they make a lovely couple?" Ian's mother sidled up beside him. What he wasn't sure of is if she was referring to his cousin Finn or to Hannah.

"Yeah. They do." It was true for both couples.

His mother looped her elbow into his and started walking. "You know, there are going to be a lot of nice girls at this wedding."

Ian didn't miss how DJ rolled his eyes and smothered a laugh.

"I'm sure there will be."

"I'm serious." The smile slipped from his mom's face. "You're not getting any younger, you know. You and your brother should have found a nice girl a long time ago."

"I know, Mom." Ian shot his cousin a stop-laughing-glare over his mother's head. He loved his mom, but his line of work didn't leave a lot of time for dating, nice girls or not.

His mother blew out a resigned sigh and Ian wondered if she really could read his mind.

"At least promise me you'll ask a girl or two to dance?" she asked.

"I promise." Ian patted her arm. "And one of these days I'll find the right woman, just don't get your hopes up it will be at the reception."

"I don't care where you find her so long as she's not behind bars."

At least that was one promise he should easily be able to keep.

MEET CHRIS

USA TODAY Bestselling Author of more than a dozen contemporary novels, including the award winning *Champagne Sisterhood*, Chris Keniston lives in suburban Dallas with her husband, two human children, and two canine children. Though she loves her puppies equally, she admits being especially attached to her German Shepherd rescue. After all, even dogs deserve a happily ever after.

More on Chris and her books can be found at
www.chriskeniston.com

Follow Chris on Facebook at ChrisKenistonAuthor
or on Twitter @ckenistonauthor

Questions? Comments?
I would love to hear from you.
You can reach me at chris@chriskeniston.com

CPSIA information can be obtained
at www.ICGtesting.com
Printed in the USA
LVHW08s0008110718
583349LV00001B/162/P